THE MARSHAL AND THE MURDERER

By the Same Author

Death in Autumn
Death in Springtime
Death of a Dutchman
Death of an Englishman

THE MARSHAL AND THE MURDERER

MAGDALEN NABB

A Marshal Guarnaccia Mystery

CHARLES SCRIBNER'S SONS

New York

Charles Scribner's Sons
Macmillan Publishing Company
866 Third Avenue, New York, NY 10022

Library of Congress Cataloging-in-Publication Data

Nabb, Magdalen, 1947–
The marshal and the murderer: a Marshal Guarnaccia
mystery / by Magdalen Nabb.—1st American ed.
    p. cm.
ISBN 0–684–18884–8
I. Title.
PR6064.A18M3   1987   87-16092
823'.914—dc19   CIP

10 9 8 7 6 5 4 3 2 1

PRINTED IN THE UNITED STATES OF AMERICA

THE MARSHAL AND THE MURDERER

CHAPTER 1

'Well, I hope I haven't taken up too much of your time . . .'
Biondini, the curator of the Palatine Gallery, blinked nervously behind his big glasses, his gaze wandering over the heads of the people ascending the great stone staircase of the Pitti Palace as though any one of them might be a picture thief.

'No, no . . .' Marshal Guarnaccia assured him placidly. 'At this time of year . . .'

'Quite frankly it's not security that's giving me a headache with this exhibition, it's whether we'll get it hung in time for the opening. The catalogue won't be ready, that's a certainty by now, and as for staffing the place over Christmas . . . well, I'll have to worry about that when I get to it—excuse me again, you don't want to hear about my problems . . .'

They had reached the bottom of the staircase where the big iron lamps were still lit around the courtyard though they did little to dispel the gloom of a foggy November morning.

'I'll leave you here, Marshal.'

The two shook hands.

'Oh, I almost forgot . . .' Biondini slid a thin hand into his inside pocket and pulled out two printed invitations. 'You will come to the opening? And do bring your wife. Now I must run, I have someone waiting to see me about that catalogue. Thank you again . . .'

He hurried back up the stairs.

Marshal Guarnaccia came out under the big stone archway and stood for a moment letting his gaze roll over the cars parked on the sloping forecourt. He was probably the only man in Florence who appreciated the dirty November weather since it allowed him to go without the sunglasses he almost always wore to protect his large, rather bulging eyes which were allergic to sunlight.

Everything looked quiet and orderly in the car park. Below it the traffic was moving steadily and only the occasional impatient hoot of a car horn punctuated the steady buzz of the city going about its winter business.

Satisfied, the Marshal turned to the right and went into the Carabinieri Station that was housed in one wing of the palace.

The narrow stairs leading up to the Station always served to remind him that he was overweight. He took them slowly, let himself in with a key and crossed the empty waiting-room to his office. He could hear a typewriter going in the duty room and an expression of weariness settled on his face at the thought that he, too, had a lot of paperwork to get through. It was Tuesday, and though he always intended to get through the pile of reports on stolen cars and minor break-ins that came in on Monday morning as an aftermath of the weekend, he somehow always found something better to do and they got left until Tuesday.

He switched on the desk lamp and sat down heavily, staring at the map of Florence on the wall in front of him. Then he reached for the first sheet on the pile.

'Marshal?'

Brigadier Lorenzini put his head round the door. 'Oh . . . you're busy. It'll keep till later if . . .'

'No, no! Come in, son, come in. Something happened?'

'Nothing much, but there was a young woman in here asking for you, it would be about half an hour ago. I suppose you were still with Dr Biondini.'

'What did she want?'

'That's just it, she wouldn't say. She asked for the Marshal and when I said you were out she said she'd come back later. The thing is, I'd swear she doesn't know you anyway —she's foreign. I think your not being here was just an excuse to change her mind, you know how some people are, they decide to make a complaint and then when they get in here . . .'

'I know. Foreign, was she? Where from?'

'Swiss, she said, but she didn't have her passport with her. In fact, it was when I asked her for it that she got nervous and left. Well, it's probably nothing, only she left me with the impression . . .'

'Well?'

'I don't know, she seemed genuinely upset about something and it kind of stuck in my mind. If there's anything in it I suppose she'll be back.'

'I suppose so. How are things at home?'

'Fine. Couldn't be better.'

They were expecting their first baby shortly and it might have been the first child to be born into this world. Lorenzini, always precipitate, had had his little Fiat overhauled three times to be ready for flight towards the hospital, the first time when his wife was only in her fifth month.

'If you wait until the lads have eaten you can go home to lunch, if you like.'

'Thanks, Marshal! I didn't like to before when she was always queasy and couldn't stand the smell of cooking but now it's passed off . . . and I like to check up, well, you never know . . .' He looked earnestly at his superior as if afraid of being laughed at, but the Marshal only looked solemnly back at him, his big eyes expressionless, and said, 'Of course. But she'll be all right, she's a fine healthy young woman.'

The truth was that he rather envied Lorenzini. When his own two boys had been born he had been here in Florence and his wife at home down in Syracuse and he'd had to content himself with a telephone call once a week.

He sighed as the door closed behind young Lorenzini. The pile of papers still lay there on the desk and it wasn't going to disappear of its own accord.

The midday bells were ringing and a good smell of meat sauce was filtering down from the lads' quarters when at last the Marshal pushed the final report away from him, muttering, 'No decent lock on the door and money lying about all over the house and then they come round whining at me as if it were my fault . . .'

The smell of that sauce woke his appetite with a sharp pang. And then he remembered that his wife had been tossing breadcrumbs in a frying-pan when he left her that morning which meant his favourite *pasta alla mollica* for lunch. The thought, plus that of the completed paperwork, cheered him, though it would be another hour and a half before the boys came hurtling across the piazza from school. He got up, thinking to go and look in on the boy who would be alone in the duty room while his mate was upstairs cooking, but then he heard voices outside the door and when he opened it he found Lorenzini there examining the passport of a girl who started and looked anxiously round as he came out. He went forward and held out his hand for the passport, looking hard at the girl whose features seemed somehow blurred behind the big glasses she wore. She must have been very short-sighted.

'You were here this morning?' he asked her, flipping through the passport.

'Yes, it's probably nothing, I don't know whether I should be bothering you . . .'

'What time did you come?'

'What time? I don't . . . I think it was about nine o'clock.'

'Nine-seventeen, Marshal,' said Lorenzini, who had since checked.

'Come this way please, Signorina—' he glanced again at the passport—'Signorina Stauffer.' The Marshal opened the door of his office and stood back to let her pass.

'Well, if you think . . .'

'Take a seat.' The Marshal seated himself on his own side of the desk and looked at her for a moment without speaking. Her light brown hair was cut short and hung smooth and close to her face so that with the glasses which enlarged and distorted her pale eyes it was almost impossible to make out what she looked like. Not only that, but she wore a dark jacket whose collar was turned up against her cheeks and she held it there with one hand, letting go of it for a second every so often to adjust her glasses, then clutching at it again.

'Perhaps you'd like to take off your coat,' the Marshal suggested.

'No, no. Thank you. I'm all right like this.'

But it was very hot in the little office.

She wasn't only very short-sighted, he decided, she was desperately shy, and fairly agitated.

'What did you want to tell me?'

'It's not about me . . . that is . . . it's about a friend of mine . . .'

'And what's happened to this friend of yours?' asked the Marshal, wondering if the friend existed. So many people came in with long rambling stories about some imaginary friend, finishing up with 'so what do you think I—he should do?' 'Your boyfriend, is it?'

'No, no, a girl. We share a flat.' The hand slid up and pushed at the glasses again, covering the face.

'So? You share a flat.' Was she ever going to get to the point? Even so, the Marshal betrayed no impatience but continued to sit with his big hands planted on the desk, observing her. Seeing that it was hopeless, that she didn't go on, he said:

'Where is this flat, the address?'

'Via delle Caldaie . . . that's just off Piazza Santo Spirito.'

'I know where it is. What number?'

'Number nine. The top floor.'

'Do you have a telephone?'

'Yes.' She gave him the number and he wrote it on the pad by the telephone just in case.

'How long have you been living there?'

'I . . . we—since the first of July when we arrived from Switzerland.'

'Police permit?'

'I didn't bring it with me, I didn't think . . .'

'Do you have one?'

'Yes. So has Monica. A three-month one that will run out in December.'

Well, they were making progress. The friend now had a name and so was probably not imaginary.

'And the motive for which these permits were granted?'

'Study. We came to study here together at the Scuola Raffaello—it was more of an extended holiday than anything but then we decided to stay even longer.'

'You like it here, do you?'

'Very much. We're still enrolled at the school although I don't pay fees any more, I help out with the secretarial work.'

'Is that the sort of work you did at home?'

'No . . . no, we're both teachers and that's what we'll go back to, I expect, if . . .' Again the hand went up to the glasses. The Marshal couldn't be sure but he thought there were tears in the girl's eyes.

'Listen, Signorina . . . I can see you're upset but if you don't tell me what it's about I can't help you, can I?'

'You probably can't anyway.'

The Marshal repressed a sigh. However, this time the girl went on without any prompting.

'I told myself I'd wait three days—I haven't even told anyone at the school—but then this morning I got panicky. She's sometimes gone off for a day but staying out overnight . . . she didn't take anything with her, you see, that's why I was—'

'So your friend's missing?'

'Of course, that's what I'm worried about.'

'Of course. When did you last see her?'

'Friday afternoon about four o'clock.'

'Then she's been missing since Friday?'

'No. At least, I suppose she could have been but I was away. We went to Rome, you see, a group of us from the school. We travelled back early Monday morning. I didn't expect to find Monica at the flat because she works in the mornings but then she didn't come back in the afternoon, or even last night to sleep—do you really think she might have been missing since Friday night?'

'How could I possibly know that, Signorina—now don't distress yourself. How old is your friend Monica?'

'Twenty-five.'

'Then she's old enough to take care of herself and to go off on a trip alone if she felt like it, isn't she?'

'She didn't take anything.' The girl's face was flushed dark with annoyance. She may have been timid but she was stubborn and stood her ground.

'If you're sure about that you should be able to tell me what she was wearing.'

'Blue jeans, a beige polo-neck sweater and a heavier, hand-knitted beige sweater over that, a long quilted jacket, red, and knee-length leather boots, her old ones. They were the clothes she went to work in. She wouldn't have gone away anywhere dressed in those clothes, they were stained.'

'Stained? What sort of job does she do?'

'She works for an artisan in the potteries.'

'Just a moment.' The Marshal drew a sheet of paper towards him. 'This girl has a permit to study here and now you tell me she works. You say she's a teacher and now it seems she's a potter. Shall we start again from the beginning?' Hadn't he heard it said that the Swiss were cold and efficient? Maybe that was the Germans . . .

'Now then. Let's leave aside her disappearance for the moment and just have the facts. What's her surname?'

'Heer. Monica Heer. Wait . . . I've brought her passport with me in case . . .'

'Right. Height 5 feet 5. Hair blonde. She's very pretty.'

'Yes.' The remark didn't seem to go down too well.

'Age twenty-five, nationality Swiss. Profession?'

'Art teacher.'

'Ah. And she's enrolled in this school, what was it again?'

'The Scuola Raffaello in Piazza della Repubblica.'

'Studying?'

'Italian. For three months we went there full time and studied Italian plus craft work in the afternoons. We chose pottery although they do leather work and woodcarving as well. I wasn't any good at it myself but Monica's very talented. When we finished the full-time course we carried on just with Italian, and Monica . . .'

'Got work with this artisan. Uninsured I suppose. Illegal.'

Was that perhaps why she'd had doubts about coming here? Her hand was clutching at the dark collar again, a square hand with short neat fingernails. And very nervous.

'It wasn't really a job . . . she was learning from him. She'd really like to set up a studio when we go home instead of going back to teaching.'

Well, she wasn't the only foreigner working here illegally. It was only too easy, and a good deal for employers wanting to avoid taking on an apprentice and paying insurance. The Marshal decided to let it drop for the moment.

'And you?'

'Me?' The girl avoided his stare. 'I'm not talented like Monica.'

'But you did this pottery course, too.'

'Just because we wanted to be together. We'd only just arrived here . . .'

'And now you're doing this secretarial work for the school —I suppose that's not a real job either?'

'No, it isn't. I help out and get my Italian tuition free.'

'Hmph.' A sudden thought struck him. 'You only got here in July and started studying Italian. In that case you're remarkably fluent.'

Not that she didn't have a thick accent. Even so . . .

'We already did speak Italian. A lot of the children we teach at home are the children of Italian immigrant workers. That's what gave us the idea of coming in the first place.'

'What language do you speak at home?'

'German.'

'Both of you?'

'Yes. We're from the same Canton, Berne.'

'I see.'

The Marshal thought for a moment. Missing children were one thing, cut and dried, you knew where you were. But missing adults were another. It might want looking into and it might not. This girl was a bit strange with her funny way of hiding behind her glasses and her coat collar, but she seemed serious enough and worried enough too.

'This place where she worked, do you know where it is?'

'Of course. I was with her when she got the job—I mean when she first went there. It's not really in the potteries but just before you get there on the left-hand side of the main road. There's nothing much there except this studio that's been set up in part of a peasant's cottage, and a small factory nearby that makes terracotta ware.'

'Who's the owner of this studio?'

'His name's Berti.'

'You don't know his Christian name?'

'No. I don't know exactly what the address is either.'

'Is there a telephone there?'

'No, otherwise I'd have called right away when she didn't come home on Monday afternoon. As it is . . .'

'Yes?'

'When I'd been here this morning I decided to go there.'

'You did? It's quite a way. Do you have a car?!'

'No. I got the bus that Monica always got. I wasn't sure where to get off and I went past the place and had to walk back . . .'

'Well, had she been to work?'

'He said not. That he hadn't seen her since she left after lunch on Friday.'

'She stayed there to lunch?'

'He paid for her to eat in the restaurant in the town nearby. It's true that it wasn't really a job—I mean he paid for her lunch and her travelling expenses and sometimes if he sold one of her pieces he'd—'

'We needn't go into that now. If he hasn't seen your friend

since Friday, then don't you think that makes it likely she's gone away somewhere and will soon turn up?'

'She was wearing her working clothes,' the girl persisted.

'All right.' He took a small card from one of the desk drawers. 'Here's my telephone number. If your friend turns up let me know.'

He stood up. The girl didn't move.

'Aren't you going to do anything?'

'I'm going to get my colleagues out there to check up on whether she was seen at work yesterday and I'll circulate a description of her. There's very little else I can do, Signorina.' He opened the door for her. She kept her head down as she passed through, murmuring 'Thank you' under her breath.

Feeling rather sorry for this odd stubborn creature, the Marshal placed a fatherly hand on her shoulder as they approached the outer door.

'Don't worry too much. I'm sure she'll turn up.'

But far from appreciating his gesture the girl flinched and hurried off down the stairs without another word.

Back in his office the Marshal sat down heavily in his chair and pondered a moment before dialling the number of Borgo Ognissanti Headquarters and asking for Captain Maestrangelo, his commanding officer. Maestrangelo made a note of the girl's particulars but pointed out:

'She's over eighteen.'

'Yes. But it seems she left home in her working clothes taking nothing else with her, so . . .'

'I see . . .' The Captain didn't hesitate for long; over the years he had come to know Guarnaccia well enough to trust his instincts better than he trusted his own. 'Well, if you think it necessary you could take a look out there, maybe have a word with the local man.'

'Pieri, isn't it?'

'Pieri? No, he died, hadn't you heard?'

'No . . .'

'Heart attack, about a year ago. There's a new marshal

there, a good sort. Have a word with him. No doubt he'll
be able to tell you something about this potter she worked
for—what did you say his name was?'

'Berti! I'll say I know him. What a character!'
    'You mean he's got a record?'
    'No, no!' The Marshal's colleague in the potteries was
roaring into the telephone with such gusto that the Marshal
had to hold the receiver well away from his ear. To judge
by his accent, the new marshal was a Roman and certainly
the most cheerful-sounding character he'd ever come across.
What on earth did he find so funny?
    'Ladies' man—and at his age! But some of them never
give up. He's well known about these parts.'
    'Is he? Well, I don't like the sound of that because the
reason I'm ringing you is that there's a young Swiss girl
who's been working for him, probably illegally, and she
seems to be missing.'
    'Blonde girl, nice-looking?'
    'That's right. You know her?'
    'Of course I know her! She picked a bad one to work for
there—not that there's any real harm in him but even so I
told her to watch out. She reckons she can look after herself
but these foreign lasses are sometimes a bit naïve. Pretty,
though, very pretty!'
    'How exactly did you come across her?'
    'In the restaurant. Everyone eats there including us as
we've no canteen. You'll see if you pay us a visit—are you
thinking of coming out here?'
    'I don't know . . . it's out of my area. On the other hand,
the girl lives in this Quarter so I thought I ought to look
into the thing. Her friend who shares a flat with her seems
to think she must have left for work on Monday morning
since the only clothes missing are her work clothes. You
didn't see her yesterday by any chance?'
    'No. Yesterday no. I was there at my usual table but she
didn't come in. I remember remarking on it at the time

because it's some months she's been coming and I don't think she's often missed before. She wasn't there today, either.'

'Then I suppose she didn't go to work after all unless something happened to her on the way—you couldn't be mistaken, could you? Is it a big restaurant?'

'Big? It's big all right! As I said everybody eats there, but I couldn't be mistaken because she always sat with us, Tozzi, the owner, insisted on it. She always came in alone, you see, and the place is full of workmen—you don't often get a woman in there except the occasional buyer who's been round the factories. No, I'd say I'm not mistaken.'

'What about this man Berti? If she worked for him didn't he eat with her?'

'Not him! He has to go home for lunch. His wife's up to all his tricks, she's no fool. He used to drop her off in the car and go on home.'

'Well, you never know, maybe he managed to slip the leash yesterday and take her somewhere else to lunch.'

'He'd never get away with that in a small place like this —mind you, the way he used to look at her when he thought she wasn't noticing, the old rogue!'

The Marshal thought for a moment and then said: 'I think I will pay you a visit . . .'

'Delighted to hear it! We'll be here—we never close! Filthy weather we're having and you'll find it ten times worse out here.'

But he sounded as pleased as if he were remarking on the brilliant sunshine!

'When do we expect you?'

The Marshal felt like setting out immediately, it had been a dullish day and he wouldn't have minded spending an hour with this man who seemed to be bursting with cheerfulness. Even so, he said: 'Tomorrow morning. It might be a good idea if I came on the bus she caught and ask if anyone saw her yesterday.'

'Good idea, good idea! Now, what I can do for you is to

go along and see what our friend Berti has to say for himself, nose around the area, how would that be?'

'Thank you,' said the Marshal uncertainly, 'but perhaps it would be better if you didn't say—'

The other roared with laughter. 'Don't you worry about that! I won't tell him a thing, soul of discretion, that's me! Pass the time of day and have a look at his pots—might say I'm looking for something for the wife's birthday. Crafty! Trip out in this filthy fog is just what I need! Be seeing you, then. All the best!'

When he'd hung up the Marshal leaned back in his big chair and gave a tiny satisfied belch. He'd eaten too much lunch yet again. Every day he swore he wouldn't, but after all those grass widower years of snatching a bit of bread and cheese the pleasure of going through to his quarters to be greeted by a warm smell of cooking and the comfortable noise of the children was too good to resist and he always ate with relish. Now his eyelids were smarting and heavy and he could feel that his face was flushed in the hot little room. For two pins he'd have fallen asleep there and then.

This wouldn't do. His head jerked up and he blinked. This wouldn't do at all. Now what had he meant to see to . . .?

The bus, that was what he needed to know. He dialled the number that was written on the telephone pad. It only rang once before the receiver was snatched up at the other end.

'Monica, is that you?'

'Signorina Stauffer? This is Marshal Guarnaccia speaking.'

'Oh . . .' She was evidently disappointed but she added anxiously, 'Have you found out something?'

'It's a bit soon for that, Signorina, but tomorrow I'm going to visit the place where your friend Monica worked and I'd like you to tell me what time she caught the bus out of Florence so that I can ask the other passengers if they saw her yesterday, do you understand?'

'Yes. All right. She caught the eight twenty-five.'

'Always?'

'Yes . . . You get off at the last stop before the town and you'll see the place right there on the roadside to your left. Do you think something's happened to her?'

'I've no reason to think that at this stage.'

'Something has, I can feel it. She would never . . . Thank you for trying to help.'

Again he felt sorry for her but before he could say anything comforting she suddenly hung up. What a strange creature. He decided he'd better have another cup of coffee. Even then it was an hour before he felt really awake again and he swore to himself that tomorrow he would eat less. Then he remembered that in all likelihood he'd end up in that restaurant with his cheery colleague and got to wondering what the food would be like there.

'Viareggio and Forte dei Marmi, bay number two. Viareggio and Forte dei Marmi . . .'

The fluorescent lighting in the bus station waiting-room only made everything look even dirtier. Outside it was drizzling steadily and the city looked grey, even the soaked grass around the concrete station building opposite. The Marshal was sitting on a hard bench surrounded by the smell of wet clothing, and to make matters worse the fat woman next to him kept giving her umbrella a shake so that drips of water rolled from it down the trousers of his uniform. The espresso machine on the bar at one end of the room added its steam to the general dampness and the fug of cigarette smoke. A man in a dirty overall was sweeping up cigarette ends and biscuit wrappings from the wet floor. How could anyone be going to the seaside in November and on a day like this? And yet two or three people got up when the Viareggio bus was announced and went out to the departure bays where the blue buses waited. Maybe they lived there . . . or worked there or had someone to visit there . . .

'*Bay number six, Lastra a Signa, Ponte a Signa, Montelupo, Empoli, Fucecchio. Bay number six . . .*'

That was the one. It was already eight twenty-five and the driver was aboard with the engine going. The Marshal waited to let everyone else get on so that he could have a word with the driver without blocking the queue. The last to get on was the fat woman who managed to give the Marshal a poke with her wet umbrella as she pushed past him and heaved herself up the steps.

'Help yourself,' the driver said as he switched on his windscreen wipers. Trails of dirty water ran down on each side of them. 'Filthy morning.'

The bus was only half full. The Marshal clipped his ticket in the machine and squeezed himself into a window seat as the bus bounced along a wide road leading out of the city. Once they were out of the heavy traffic the driver switched a radio on and loud music from some local radio station drowned the buzz of conversation that had started up as soon as they were under way. The Marshal took the Swiss passport out of his pocket and squeezed his way out again.

He took the passengers one by one, leaning over their seats and showing them the photograph inside the passport. They were all women except for one elderly man in a shabby raincoat and a greasy black beret. As he had judged from the way they had all started chattering even between separate seats, most of them were regulars and had seen the girl. Unfortunately there was some disagreement as to whether she had been on the bus on Monday.

'It's no use asking me,' said the woman with the umbrella with some satisfaction, 'I only go Wednesdays and Fridays to see my sister in the hospital.'

Somebody sniggered.

'What's there to laugh about? Disgusting, that's what it is, laughing at other people's misfortunes!' And she turned to the window, rubbed a patch in the steam with a brown woollen glove and stared out at the rain, tight-lipped.

Somebody prodded the Marshal in the back and he

turned. It was the old man in the greasy beret.

'What she means,' he whispered so that the Marshal had to bend over to hear him above the noise of the radio, 'is that she goes to see her sister in the asylum.' He broke off cackling, 'And she isn't the only one on this bus . . . I'm going there myself, if you want to know, to see my son who's never been right in the head. With his mother gone, you see, there was nobody to see to him and he got into trouble—well, it's better than prison—but that madam's the only one who calls it a hospital. You mark my words, her sister's as mad as a hatter and if you ask me she's not much better herself.'

The Marshal looked around him, his eyes bulging more than usual.

'You mean all these people . . .?'

'Oh, not all of them but a good part. You mark my words—but they'll not all admit it.'

'And what about you?'

'I've told you, my son . . .'

'No, I mean do you recognize this photograph?'

'I recognize it all right. A pretty thing, isn't she? What's happened to her?'

'I don't know. Did you see her on Monday?'

'I wasn't on the bus Monday. Wednesdays and Fridays, same as her ladyship there. Why don't you ask the driver?'

The people who had been on the bus on Monday were still arguing loudly.

'She was sitting right in front of me!'

'No, you're wrong. She was on the bus but right at the front.'

The Marshal pushed his way forward along the narrow aisle and signalled to the driver to turn the radio down.

'I want a word with you when you stop.'

'Right you are.'

They were well out of Florence and following the river and the electric railway line in the direction of Pisa, passing through a series of small towns that looked depressing in the rain. In the centre of one of them the bus stopped and the driver looked up.

'What can I do for you?'

'I'm trying to trace this girl. Do you know if she was on the bus on Monday morning?'

'Yes, she was.'

'You're quite sure?' By this time it seemed too good to be true. 'You saw her on Monday morning?'

'That's right.'

'It couldn't have been last Friday?'

'No, it couldn't. I was on afternoons last week. She caught this bus every morning, has done for a while. And on Monday she did her usual trick of getting up too late for her stop—there's nothing along that road until you come round a big bend and the stop's right there. She was always missing it and I often let her off well past the stop though I shouldn't. Otherwise she'd have to get off in the town and walk back. It's quite a way and it's a dangerous road with no pavement.'

'I see. Thanks. In that case you'd better warn me when we get to her stop or I'll be doing the same myself.'

'Will do.'

He turned up the radio again and the Marshal swayed back to his seat. His damp trouser legs were getting hot and itchy from the blast of the bus's heaters. He rubbed a big patch on the steamy window as the other passengers had all done.

The small towns had petered out and they were travelling between wet fields and ghostly orchards. The rain and fog were getting increasingly heavy so perhaps his cheery colleague hadn't been joking about the weather being ten times worse out here. Probably it was the proximity to the river. On the right, the railway was now hidden behind a dripping high black wall and only the overhead wires were visible. The bus picked up speed and big lorries with their headlights on came roaring towards them out of the gloom from the direction of the industrial towns ahead. The driver was right, it was a dangerous road and had no doubt had its share of fatal accidents.

The bus swished round a broad curve and slowed to a stop, apparently in the middle of nowhere.

'Here you are, chief!'

The Marshal climbed down. 'Thanks.'

'You're welcome.'

He had almost to flatten himself against the wet wall as the bus pulled away and then was forced to stay there for some time as lorries and a few cars streamed past in either direction. He could see a huddled little building on the other side with a patch of dirt surrounded by junk and plastic bags beside it, just wide enough for the light blue car that was parked there. By the time he managed to get across the road his hat and greatcoat were quite wet. It was obvious that, as the girl had said, this had once been an ordinary peasant's cottage and it had probably stood in a pretty deserted spot until this road had been constructed to serve the new factories. The biggish window on the left which was covered with torn brown paper must be the artisan's workshop. Light was showing through the tears. To the right, a woman's face appeared for a moment behind the ragged curtain of a tiny, barred window and vanished again. Out of curiosity he approached this window and peered into the gloom. At first he couldn't make out anything but he could hear the soft crowing of hens and a vague scuffling noise. A tiny black cat jumped on to the inside windowsill and rubbed itself against the wet bars. There was no glass, just the bit of ragged curtain which hung crookedly. The smell of animal excrement was almost overpowering. After a while he managed to make out the beady eyes of the hens as they paused in their scratching and pecking to observe him in case he might be the bearer of more food. The scuffling noise must be coming from inside a wine barrel. A pair of long ears flashed every so often above its rim and he gathered it must be a hare being fattened.

'There's nothing very interesting in there.'

The Marshal turned. The artisan was standing in his doorway watching him, a small paintbrush in his hand.

'Just curious.' The Marshal looked him up and down, a little surprised to see that he was wearing a grey mohair suit that had once been quite good though now it was worn and rather dusty. Perhaps he had taken his overall off, seeing someone approach. The Marshal was quite sure that he kept an eye on the goings-on on the road through the tears in the paper. 'It was you I came to see. Your name's Berti?'

'That's right. Don't you want to come in out of the rain?'

'I wouldn't mind.' He followed Berti, a much shorter man than himself and rather scraggy, into the workshop.

'I must be disturbing you . . .'

Berti shrugged. 'People come in all the time.'

A paraffin stove was hissing in the oblong room which was bigger than the Marshal had expected. Every inch of wall space was taken up with majolica plates and the place was crammed with pottery of every description, some of it on crooked dusty shelves and makeshift tables and a lot of it on the stone floor so that the Marshal hardly dared move for fear of breaking something.

'I'll get you a chair,' Berti said, and picked his way through it all easily to the back of the room, where he shifted a stack of dishes from a dusty chair which he carried back with him without dislodging so much as an eggcup from the jumble.

'Thanks.'

'Don't sit down yet . . .' He dusted the chair off with a bit of rag. 'That's the best I can do but you'll find it'll brush off all right.'

Berti sat down himself at what must have been his habitual place by the window. A small table beside him was crammed with pots of colour and brushes of various shapes and sizes and more similar pots stood about the floor at his feet. The Marshal, who would have immediately crushed or knocked over the whole lot, was amazed by the man's delicacy which seemed so effortless and unconsidered. It was his habit when finding himself in a new place to wander around it getting his bearings, rather like a dog roaming about and sniffing in corners in an unfamiliar house, but in this place he decided he had better keep still or he'd find himself paying for any number of breakages.

'Don't you want to look round?' Berti might have been reading his thoughts though he didn't look up from his work.

'I'm all right here. Go on with your work if you like.'

In fact the artisan had already picked up a white plate and set it on a small wheel on a stand in front of him.

'You don't want to buy anything, then?'

'No, but I wouldn't mind watching you for a minute if it doesn't bother you.'

Berti shrugged as if he weren't interested either way. He spun the wheel and adjusted the plate a fraction of an inch so that it was in the centre. Then he took a loaded brush from one of the pots at his elbow and a perfect dark stripe appeared round the edge of the plate.

The Marshal, who would have loved to learn a craft but had always been too clumsy for it, watched him in silence.

'You're not from round here?' Berti commented, changing his brush and tracing another stripe, as thin as a hair, inside the first one.

'No.'

'Friend of Niccolini's?'

'Niccolini?'

'The Marshal down the road.'

'Ah . . .' He hadn't thought to ask his cheery colleague's name. 'You could say that.'

'He was in here yesterday looking for something for his wife.'

The Marshal didn't answer but glanced involuntarily at the covered window, which meant that this was a workshop with no licence to sell directly to the public.

'Eh, this is Italy, Marshal, this is Italy . . .' The artisan paused in his work to fix the Marshal with a beady, rather watery eye and the Marshal remembered his colleague's description of him as an old rogue. He was certainly an unprepossessing creature, rather spider-like, but he could well have been good-looking as a young man. His wizened features were very even and his grey hair so abundantly thick and wavy as to make him look almost top-heavy. He turned and selected another brush, twirling its point between his thin fingers.

'Niccolini didn't buy anything . . .' He dipped the brush into a pale yellow liquid and made a series of what seemed to the Marshal to be random strokes on the white surface of the plate. 'And you don't want to buy anything either. Are you going to tell me what it's all about? I'm curious, very curious.'

The Marshal cleared his throat and placed his hands squarely on his knees, only to find that they left dusty white marks. He tried to brush them away but only succeeded in spreading them.

'Something and nothing,' he said slowly, 'probably turn out to be nothing at all. I believe there's a young woman comes here in the mornings, Swiss girl . . .'

The small watery eyes darted a glance at him but the Marshal, though aware of it, didn't meet them. He kept his gaze fixed on the still incomprehensible brushstrokes.

'What about her?'

'She isn't here today?'

'No.'

'Was she here yesterday?'

'She's free to come and go as she pleases. She doesn't work for me. I told that to her little friend who came here looking for her—I suppose she was the one who brought you in?'

'Was she here?'

'The little friend?'

'Monica Heer.'

'Yesterday, no.'

'Monday?'

'Monday . . .'

'Well?'

'I'm trying to think.'

The brush was poised, motionless, but only for a second. Whatever was going on in this man's head didn't affect his hands, which moved in their own space and time, the habit of a lifetime's skill. The brush was attacking the plate rapidly with tiny delicate strokes of darker yellow which gave form to the mysterious paler marks so that, as if by magic, they took the shape of a variety of figures, writhing dragon-like animals and grotesque human torsoes with the lashing tails of beasts.

Berti swivelled his head round and grinned.

'Raphael,' he said. 'You know these grotesques?'

'I seem to have seen something like them before . . .'

'The frescoes in the Palazzo Vecchio.'

'I suppose that must be it.'

The thin fingers reached out for another brush and began tracing black outlines, fine as a hair, around the figures and adding tiny glaring eyes and scales.

'She wasn't here on Monday, Monica. Pretty girl. Talented too. That's her work.' He indicated a group of plates hanging on the wall by the door. The colours were more limited and the designs more abstract than the pieces surrounding it. The Marshal noted a broken dusty mirror propped on a shelf beside them. 'She has her own ideas, not like ours.'

'You teach her?'

'Technique. Her designs are nice enough but it takes years of practice before the hand becomes light enough for this work. It's really a specialized job but she wanted to learn everything about the pottery business, that's why . . .'

'That's why what?'

'That's why, if she wasn't here on Monday, she probably went to Moretti.'

'And who's Moretti?'

'He has the terracotta factory just a few yards away round the bend.'

'Why would she have gone there?'

'They're firing tomorrow.'

'And she wanted to learn about that?'

'No, no.' The plate was finished and Berti got up and placed it on a stack of others by the door with a scrap of paper under it so that it didn't touch the one below. Then he stood wiping his hands on a dusty rag. 'I see you don't know much about this business. I'll explain. At one time I used to do everything here, throwing, decorating, firing, but I gave it up a year or so ago. I'm not as young as I was and it cost me more in time and money than it was worth. It's not as though I have a son to take over from me . . . Anyway I sold my wheel and kiln and now I buy these plates in biscuit—when they've already been fired once—from a factory and I decorate them. Moretti fires them for me. It's easier and more profitable, you follow me?'

'I follow you.'

'Well, as I said, the Swiss girl wanted to learn the whole business, set up her own studio. I could only teach her majolica and that's why once or twice she's been round to Moretti's place, just to keep her hand in at throwing.'

'You said before he was firing . . .'

'That's right. That's why—I'm going round there now if you want to know more about it. You could ask him if she was there. I haven't seen her since Friday.'

'I will.' The Marshal was staring out through a tear in the paper at the bus stop against the dripping black wall opposite. 'If this Moretti's place is just round the bend I imagine she must have got off the bus here just the same. They told me there isn't another stop before the town.'

Berti's sharp little eyes followed his glance and understood.

'I don't always get here that early. You might not have found me here at this time today if I didn't have to get this stuff round to Moretti.'

'The girl always caught the bus I caught. Did you give her a key to get in?'

'I did no such thing.'

'Then what did she do if you hadn't arrived?'

'She waited.'

Again the Marshal looked out of the window at the heavy traffic streaming past under the drizzle. Had Berti noticed that they had begun to talk of the Swiss girl in the past tense? He was bending over now, dusting off his shoes with the rag. All his movements were slow, accurate and continuous. Crouched over like that, he looked more spider-like than ever.

'If you'll wait a minute I'll just open the car.'

'But if it's only round the bend . . .'

Without a word Berti pointed to the stack of plates and went out. He backed the car round to the door and opened the boot. When he came back in the Marshal said, 'Do you want some help?'

Berti only grinned slyly. 'I don't think you could manage.'

Only as Berti lifted the plates did the Marshal realize that the white surface on which the designs were painted consisted of a thick layer of fine white powder of which the brushstrokes had disturbed not a grain.

'Raw glaze. You need experience to handle it.'

When the pots were packed and the Marshal was settled in the passenger seat Berti went back to lock up. Through the rear-view mirror the Marshal saw him pause just inside the door, staring towards the wall intently, then take a comb from his pocket and run it carefully through his thick grey hair.

CHAPTER 2

They drove through the rain in silence for twenty yards or so. Berti drove very slowly and with what seemed exaggerated care, glancing every few seconds into his rearview mirror. No doubt, the Marshal thought, he was worried about breaking his plates if he had to brake suddenly.

'That's Moretti's place.' It was on the left like Berti's studio and, as he'd said, just round a curve in the road. 'I'll have to turn round here.' He drove into a lay-by in front of the gates of an enormous old house that stood well back from the road almost opposite the factory, its stuccoed façade stained dark yellow in the rain.

'Robiglio,' he remarked with a snigger, 'and his seven-lavatory mansion,' and glanced at the Marshal as he changed into first. When the Marshal offered no comment but maintained a pop-eyed silence he lifted his hand and rubbed the thumb and forefinger together. 'A millionaire.'

When a space appeared in the traffic he nosed out slowly and turned to park in front of Moretti's ramshackle factory which had a high terrace giving on to the road with steps leading up on each side of it. A big stocky man wearing a knitted cap and with a piece of sacking over his shoulders was up there heaving some bulging plastic bags about in the rain.

Berti got out of the car and called out: 'Moretti in?'

The man pointed to their left and went on heaving the bags. The Marshal got out and they climbed the wet stone steps.

'In his office,' Berti said, opening the door of what was hardly more than a shack detached from the rest of the building.

Moretti was there, standing by a trestle table littered with orders and invoices. He turned and was about to greet Berti when he saw the Marshal and remained silent.

'I've brought my stuff,' Berti said, and with a sly look at the Marshal: 'And somebody who wants a word with you.'

'What can I do for you?' Moretti was small and wiry with a shock of red hair. He looked the Marshal straight in the eye.

'Just some information. This is your factory?'

'Mine and my brother's.'

'I'm trying to trace a Swiss girl; Monica Heer. I believe she sometimes came here.'

'What of it? She wasn't working for me.' He shot an accusing glance at Berti.

'I'm not suggesting that she was, and in any case I'm not interested in who she was working for. I'm trying to trace her, that's all.'

'How do you mean, trace her? What for? If she's in trouble with you people it's nothing to do with me.'

He wasn't hostile, only brusque, but there was something aggressive or even defiant in the way he continued to look the Marshal straight in the eye.

'It seems she's missing,' put in Berti, rubbing his hands slowly together, his little eyes taking in everything in the cluttered office. 'She hasn't been seen since Friday.'

'Well, she's not here. You'd better get your stuff up there, they're more than half way through loading.' He picked up a pair of dusty reading glasses and put them on, letting them rest almost on the end of his nose as though he never wore them for long. Then he took a blue invoice from the pile as if to indicate that, as far as he was concerned, their talk was over. When the Marshal didn't follow Berti out he looked up and said: 'If there's nothing else . . . I have to have all these invoices ready by tomorrow. You'll excuse me, this is a busy few days for us.'

'That's all right,' said the Marshal blandly, 'there's nothing else . . . Except that I was wondering if she came here on Monday morning . . .'

'Monday morning . . .? I suppose she could have done since we're ready to fire.'

'She could have done? Surely you'd have seen her?'

'Not necessarily. I only came in for half an hour to talk to some buyers. I took them round a couple of other factories and then to the restaurant in town. We were in here, so for all I know she could have been inside, throwing.'

'Somebody would have seen her.'

'I doubt it, not on Monday. The point is, when we're

about to fire and the last pieces are drying out we usually take a long weekend. All my men are on piece work except the apprentice and they work all hours when we've a lot on, then take a bit of time off when we're firing. That was when the girl used to come round, to use the wheel when the throwers were off. Once everything's dry and we're ready to load the kiln everybody mucks in and helps. This is a small place, run on family lines. Monday there was nothing doing, the place was empty.'

'You mean the girl could have just walked in here? You don't lock up?'

'Lock up? No, never, there's no need . . .' Moretti ran a hand through his disordered red hair, hesitating as though embarrassed by what he had just said and wondering how to justify it. 'In a place like this there's nothing to steal . . . I do lock this office up with a bit of a padlock but I don't know why I bother since there's never any money here.'

'I see. Well, I'll let you get on, then . . .'

The Marshal decided he'd better get some background information from his cheery colleague at the Carabinieri Station in the town before getting involved any further. He always liked to sniff about on his own first, with no preconceived ideas, but these people seemed to live in a world of their own whose workings were foreign to him. Even so, when he spotted Berti carrying the last of his plates into the factory he followed him, partly in the hope that some workman in there might have been around on Monday despite what Moretti had said, and partly because he was beginning to feel certain that something had happened to the girl who, if he were to believe all he'd been told, had got off a bus outside Berti's studio and disappeared into thin air.

When he got inside the gloomy building Berti had vanished and there was no one else in sight. The place was like a maze. There was no understanding how it was constructed. So many crooked passageways, rickety wooden stairs, rooms that led into each other and brought you back to where you started from. He began to believe that the girl could have been in here without anybody knowing it. After rambling about aimlessly for some time without coming across a soul or hearing anything other than the sound of his own footsteps he found himself in a long high room that seemed almost empty, so that it was impossible to understand what normally went on there, if anything. There were windows all along one side of it, all of them dirty and one or two of them broken so that the rain was coming in. In one corner of the room stood an old bath full of bits of clay covered with water, and nearby a box containing coils of thick wire. Then a great empty stretch and at the far end a group of large white shapes. The Marshal approached them, curious, but even seeing them close up he was none the wiser. Huge plaster shells, rough on the outside and smooth on the inside. He touched one of them tentatively. It was damp and very cold. Then he heard muffled voices coming from directly beneath him and started down the nearest staircase. On the floor below there was no one and he was obliged to wander through three or four other rooms before finding his way down to the next floor, losing himself and the spot the voices came from. At last he heard them again and entered a room almost as big as the one two floors above. But this one was full and busy. In the centre of it was a huge kiln with piles of broken bricks and what looked like some sort of crumbling red cement around its gaping mouth. The rest of the room was filled with row upon row of dark, big-bellied pots, many of them almost as tall as the two men who were lifting them one by one and carrying them to the mouth of the kiln. One of the men looked up without interrupting his movements.

'If you're looking for the boss, he's in his office.'

'No.' The Marshal stepped back out of their path. 'I was looking for Signor Berti.'

The man nodded in the direction of the kiln. The Marshal waited until they had deposited their burden and then went nearer and peered into the gloom. A boy was crouched inside the entrance sorting through piles of biscuit-coloured tubes and fitting castellated tops on to them. Behind the boy, Berti was passing his plates through to some chamber beyond from which muffled voices issued.

'That's the lot?'

'Two more.'

'Saggar's full!'

'I'll pass you a shelf.'

'The boss won't like it . . .'

'He won't know.'

'He'll know if he sees as much as one spot of glaze on any of his stuff . . .'

Ignoring the complaining voice, Berti came forward to the crouching boy. 'Give me four props and a shelf . . .' Then he saw the dark figure of the Marshal blocking the light at the kiln's entrance, as round and heavy as the jars piling up around him. 'You'll get yourself dirty there. I'll be out in a minute.'

Indeed, the Marshal on glancing down at his black greatcoat found that there were large patches of iron red dust on it. Nevertheless, he stayed where he was. He was feeling uneasy and instead of asking questions as he had intended he went on standing there, observing everything with big troubled eyes. In any case, he was convinced that if anybody here had something to hide these people would stick together like a family. You could tell it even from the way they worked, or rather went on working. Usually when a uniformed carabiniere appeared in a place unexpectedly, however innocuous the visit, it had the effect of breaking up whatever was going on if only for the sake of curiosity, but here his presence had no effect at all. He wasn't one of them and so didn't matter. In the end all he asked of the two men lining up the big jars by the kiln was: 'How many of you work here?'

'Counting the boss?'

'If you like.'

'Eight, then. There's a hairline crack in the rim of that

one.' Already he had turned away to concentrate on the job in hand. 'No—the one beyond . . . that's it. Give it a rub down, will you, and let's hope it doesn't open up in the fire.' Then he did turn back to the Marshal but only to say, 'I'll have to ask you to move, do you mind?'

'No, no . . .' He backed up as carefully as he could and was glad to see Berti emerging with his slow, spidery steps from the kiln.

'Well, did you find out whether she was here?'

'No.'

Berti picked up a bit of rag from a dusty windowsill and wiped his hands. There was a strip of wood lying on the sill with four or five little figures on it modelled in red clay. One of them was a crudely worked head with spiky hair and big ears, the mouth no more than a gaping hole. Berti picked it up and sniggered. 'Looks like Moretti.' He set it down again with as much care as if it had been one of his own pieces.

Perhaps the apprentice had made the things. The Marshal was no judge but he reckoned the boy was about fifteen and a bit old for such childish work, unless it was a joke. It was true that the comical head bore a strong resemblance to the factory boss.

'Shall we go?' The Marshal had no intention of trying to find his way out of the maze without Berti. He was annoyed to find that after only two turnings they were out in the rain again.

Moretti nodded to them without a word as they passed the open door of his office shack and went down the steps, ducking their heads against the rain. The man with the woollen hat and the sacking round his shoulders was still heaving the big plastic bags, some of which had burst and were oozing smooth red clay. His huge wet hands were red with cold.

They got into the car. Almost opposite, a white Mercedes was nosing slowly out at the gates of the big house and the driver was peering fixedly over the steering-wheel at them. 'There he is,' sniggered Berti, 'and you can bet your life he needs those seven lavatories, he's so full of—'

'I'd be grateful if you could give me a lift into the town.'
The Marshal found Berti more than a little repellent but he
didn't fancy a walk along that busy road in such filthy
weather. 'Though I shouldn't be keeping you from your
work.'

'There's always time for work. It's only five minutes of a
drive.'

He started the engine and without looking at the Marshal
added: 'You mustn't mind Moretti. He's a bit of a rough
diamond but he's a worker. And in any case he's had a hard
life . . .'

The Marshal made no comment. As they drove away he
looked back, through the raindrops dribbling down the car
windows. Up on the terrace the man with the sack round
his shoulders had stopped work and was staring after them,
grinning.

On their short journey to the town centre they passed a
number of factories as small as Moretti's, though many of
them were built of new red brick, and the landscape seemed
to the Marshal to consist of nothing but row upon row of
wet orange pots that appeared luminous against a livid sky.

''Morning, everybody! 'Morning . . . 'morning. How are
things? 'Morning . . . Tozzi! Good morning to you! I've
brought a visitor, colleague of mine from Florence, so I hope
you're going to feed us well . . . Signora Tozzi, how are you?
I'm fine myself, never better, never better! This is Marshal
Guarnaccia from Florence—ah! Now, that's what I call a
roast, look at that! Filthy day! We're frozen. Never been so
glad to see a roaring fire.'

A big open log fire was set in the middle of the restaurant's
kitchen which was the centre of frenetic activity at this busy
lunch-hour. Despite the coming and going of waiters and
the harassed cooks with red shining faces, Niccolini, the
Marshal of the little pottery town, insinuated his big athletic
figure, conspicuous in its black uniform, into the fray and

took off his leather gloves to warm himself at the fire where beefsteaks and pork chops were sizzling and spitting. Marshal Guarnaccia remained on the other side of one of the two counters that gave on to the dining-rooms.

'Come on in, Guarnaccia! Come in here and warm up— is that minestrone in that steaming cauldron? It is. We'll have a bowlful of that for a start, get the blood circulating . . .'

But the Marshal remained where he was, looking about him, until he was rescued by the proprietor, Tozzi, who came towards him wiping his hands on a clean cloth. A tall, severe-looking man with iron grey moustaches and a decidedly military bearing.

'Giuseppe Tozzi. Pleased to meet you, Marshal.'

'Guarnaccia.' The Marshal shook his hand.

'Now then . . .' Tozzi looked briskly round the restaurant like a general about to give battle orders. 'Our marshal eats in the main dining-room as a rule but I'm wondering—' He turned to address Niccolini who was pottering about the kitchen and looking into all the bubbling pans without pausing in his cheery monologue. The Marshal noticed that the people bustling around him looked cheered by his presence. It evidently didn't bother anybody, least of all Niccolini himself, that nobody had time to answer him.

'Where would you like to eat?' Tozzi called to him. 'Your usual table?'

'Fine, fine!'

'I thought you might want a bit of peace, that is if you want to talk.'

'Why not, why not? Good idea. Anything you like.'

'I'll put you in the back room, then.'

'Fine. Perfect. Anything will suit me.'

'This way, please,' said Tozzi to Guarnaccia.

The Marshal was rather sorry not to eat in the big room which had looked so bright and welcoming when they had come in from the cold and the wet, with its blue checked tablecloths each with a local pottery vase full of painted daisies in the centre and the chattering workmen tackling huge bowls of spaghetti. He followed Tozzi into a smaller and more sedate dining-room where the furniture was heavy and antique in style and the walls were covered with large majolica plates. Here well-dressed clients were talking in polite undertones as they ate.

'Let me take your coat. I put the factory owners and their buyers in here,' explained Tozzi, holding a chair for the Marshal. 'You'll be quieter. Take a look at my collection. The antique pieces are genuine.'

Left alone, the Marshal gazed about him at the big decorated plates on the walls, wondering which were the antique pieces and wishing he were in the big noisy room where he could look at the people instead. Niccolini appeared at the counter behind the bowls of freshly cooked vegetables lined up there.

'All settled in? Good. I'll be right with you!'

By the time they were half way through their bowls of minestrone the Marshal's face was as red and shining as those of the cooks working around the blazing fire. The sudden warmth of the restaurant and the thick steaming soup were all too effective after a morning spent in the cold rain. Most of the time he ate in silence, his big eyes fixed on Niccolini who managed to continue his hearty monologue while making short work of the minestrone.

'And now you've talked to Berti you see what I mean. A right character but no real harm in him, as I said. Even so, it wouldn't suit me to have a daughter of mine work there alone with him—not that I've got a daughter, two sons, one of them doing his military service with us now. What do you think of our restaurant? Tozzi does a good job, always feeds us well and it's a godsend for me because my wife works, teaches full time in Empoli, so she's never home before three. But you eat well here, very well. Ah, it's a good life if you know how to enjoy it, I always say. What about you, Guarnaccia, eh? I can see you like your food too. I've told Tozzi to bring us a few good slices off that roast—let me give you another drop of wine.'

'I don't think . . .' The Marshal's face was getting redder than ever. He was sure that if he drank any more of this good red wine he would fall asleep on the bus back to Florence. A fine figure to cut, and in uniform, too. But Niccolini had filled his glass up to the brim for him and Tozzi had rolled his trolley to the table and was carving thick juicy slices off the roast. Well, he wouldn't have any sweet, he decided, as the big plate was set before him.

'Mmm . . .!' Niccolini sat back a little later, dabbing with his napkin. 'Well, what do you think?'

'It's very good.'

'Eh? Oh, the roast? Splendid stuff. I meant what do you think about this business of the girl. Anything in it, would you say?'

'There might be, there might not. To tell you the truth, I'm more interested in what you think. After all, you know her. I've never seen her.'

'I suppose you're right. Well, she seems a sensible enough lass to me.'

'Not the sort to just drift off without telling anybody?'

'I'd say she wasn't. You never can tell, of course, I've known some strange things happen in my time, but she certainly seems very serious about what she's doing, you know what I mean? And then the Swiss, very precise people, very precise.'

'They can't all be alike,' said the Marshal reasonably.

'No, no . . . But she is precise, you see, in her ways. Careful about what she eats, too. Not enough to keep a bird alive, in my opinion, and never more than one glass of wine, though I always offer her some of mine. One glass and then mineral water. Tac! Won't be persuaded to another drop at any price.'

The Marshal, having experienced something of Niccolini's steam-roller methods of persuasion, thought this Swiss girl must be a very strong character indeed.

'She's not involved with any man around here that you know of?'

'Not that I know of, no. You can bet your life that Berti's tried, the old goat, but I can't see a pretty young girl as bright as she is having anything to do with him. My young brigadier's got a bit of a soft spot for her, too, between ourselves. He generally eats with me here and his eyes always light up when she comes in—can't blame him either. Oh, I'm not saying she encourages him, not in any serious way, but she flirts with him a bit, you know. Always looks pleased to see him, interested in everything he has to say, teases him a bit. But nothing out of place and of course I'm always here . . . Lovely girl—though it wouldn't do to be that open and friendly with the men hereabouts, in my opinion. I suppose these young foreign girls have different ways from ours . . . Even so, they're a likely bunch of lads in there.' He indicated the big room next door from where sounds of noisy talk and laughter filtered through to their sedate dining-room. 'That's why Tozzi always has her eat with us.'

'I would have thought,' said the Marshal, looking about him, 'that he'd have put her in here.'

'He would do but she won't hear of it. She reckons it's more cheerful next door with the potters, more lively. True, of course.'

'Yes.' The Marshal wished he'd had this girl's presence of mind. He'd have learnt a lot more about the town if he, too, had insisted on being next door with the potters. Well, he would have to content himself with what Niccolini could tell him. No doubt he knew everything about everybody.

'How long have you been here?'

'Just over a year. Seems like less but it was a year last month. Settled down into the woodwork right away, never miss Rome at all. Mind you, anywhere suits me, I take life as it comes. The wife had a bit of trouble settling in, changing schools and what have you, but with a bit of effort . . . an odd lot, the people round here, until you get used to them but they're good enough at heart. We get on pretty well, all in all.'

'Odd in what way?'

'Well, they are what they are, you know, they have their own ways, and you get one or two real oddities. Between you and me—' he lowered his voice—'in a place as small as this and with so many family businesses you get no fresh blood. It's all a bit too enclosed. Good in some ways, of course, because there's plenty of work here and plenty of money to be made, too. There's no need for young ones to leave home looking for work like in the South, you understand.'

'I understand.' The Marshal, who came from Sicily, knew that problem only too well.

'But on the other hand there's the fact that they marry among themselves, sometimes, not to put too fine a point on it, for business reasons as much as anything else. More than half the people in this town are related in one way or another.'

'And that leads to a lot of family quarrels?'

'No, I wouldn't say that. No. It's a very close-knit community, very close-knit.'

The Marshal remembered Moretti's factory and the feeling of being an outsider. 'That's what I felt,' he said, frowning. 'That if they felt threatened by anything from outside they'd stick together.'

'And you're quite right. You've understood exactly!'

'I felt it when I was at Moretti's place. Did you know the Swiss girl sometimes goes there?'

'Does she? No, I hadn't heard that and I wouldn't have believed it.'

'Why not?'

'Well, Berti's one thing, a sly old beggar if ever there was one, and it's not the first time he's had somebody working for him illegally—of course there's nobody to carry on his business after what happened to his son and there'd be no point in taking on an apprentice now.'

'He had a son, then?'

'Oh yes. Tragic business, tragic. Killed outright in a road accident practically under his father's eyes just outside the workshop. Must have been just before I arrived here, I remember everybody was still talking about it. Hit by a lorry coming round the curve. He was on a moped, hadn't a chance.'

Was that the reason why Berti drove the way he did and not because of the plates, as the Marshal had thought?

'Well, fancy, Moretti . . . I wouldn't have thought it of him. They say he's always been absolutely straight, one of the few. I can't see him running the risk of taking on an uninsured worker, though I don't know him well enough to be categorical. He's one who keeps himself to himself . . . never eats here, for instance, unless he brings a buyer. You're sure you're not mistaken?'

'Quite sure. Moretti himself told me. But I've given you the wrong impression, even so. She's only been there a couple of times, she certainly isn't working for him. Apparently she goes to work on the wheel when his throwers are off, which seems to be when they have enough stuff ready for firing their kiln.'

'I see. That's right, these small places generally take a long weekend . . . Well, that's different. So she goes there, does she? And is that where you think she was Monday? You were telling me back at the Station that Berti said she wasn't with him.'

'That's what he says, but it might be true and it might not.'

'Mm.'

'You wouldn't believe him?'

Niccolini roared with laughter. 'That one could hide behind a spiral staircase! Oh, I'm not saying he's necessarily lying but he would if he needed to. There's no real harm in the man, as I said before, only he may have smelled trouble and be wanting to keep out of it. If he thinks something's happened to the girl . . .'

'If something has happened to her he's going the wrong way about keeping out of trouble by lying to us.'

'People haven't much sense—let me fill your glass and no protests, this is good honest wine and can only do you good—and people who think they're crafty often have less sense than the rest. Berti thinks he's crafty and no doubt he is in his own little way and with his own kind. You probably gathered that for yourself.'

'I don't know what to think of him, to be honest.'

'Well, if she had to be in one place or the other, since you say she got off the bus as usual, my money'd be on Moretti as far as who's telling the truth goes, knowing Berti as I do.'

'And mine. But he couldn't tell me anything for sure. He says he was only there for half an hour himself and that then he went out with some clients, ending up here for lunch —we might check that while we're here. The rest of the men had the day off, so . . .'

'Mm . . . difficult.'

'It seems she could have gone in there since he never locks the place up.'

'No . . .? Ah, Signora Tozzi, you've arrived at just the right moment. You don't happen to remember if Moretti was in here Monday, do you? I didn't see him myself but then he'd have eaten in here because he'd clients with him.'

'That's right. He always eats at home otherwise. They were sitting where you're sitting now. Why?'

'No reason, no reason. You're sure it was Monday?'

'Certain. He telephoned me to book a table—there aren't that many in here so there isn't always one free. Now, I'm not going to ask you what you want for sweet—' she smiled at them, hands on her broad hips over which her clean white overall was stretched tightly—'because I've made a *torta della nonna*.'

'Oh! Signora Tozzi, you're a marvel.'

'I don't think . . .' began the Marshal.

'Oho, Guarnaccia! You're going to enjoy this. You haven't lived until you've tried Signora Tozzi's *torta della nonna*—

give him plenty, now, don't stint! Engine can't run without petrol!'

She served them two large helpings and stood over them smiling as they ate. The Marshal had to admit, in all honesty and with his mouth full, that it was exceptionally good.

'Now what about a liqueur with your coffee,' suggested the proprietress, beaming with pleasure at their appreciation, 'it's on the house.'

'No, no,' said the Marshal quickly. 'Thank you, no.'

'No,' agreed Niccolini with sudden solemnity, 'it doesn't do to exaggerate. No, that's it, that's enough.'

The Marshal sighed with inward relief.

'Or a grappa? A drop of that special grappa you tried the other day? There's still a bit left in the bottle.'

'Ah, now that's another story.' Niccolini's face brightened. 'A drop of grappa never did anybody any harm.'

'Well said!' declared a forceful voice at the Marshal's shoulder. 'Bring these gentlemen the bottle. They're my guests.'

'Oh, Signor Robiglio . . .' The proprietress pushed the sweet trolley aside hastily. 'Now where am I going to put you—there isn't a single table free.'

'Don't worry, Signora, don't worry. All in good time. No doubt there'll soon be a place, and with Marshal Niccolini's permission I shall sit here for a moment.'

'Help yourself, help yourself!'

Niccolini's voice was as loud and hearty as ever but there was an emptiness in his apparent enthusiasm that caused the Marshal to fix his big eyes on him rather than on the newcomer until the latter commanded his attention by introducing himself.

'Ernesto Robiglio. My pleasure.'

'Guarnaccia.'

Robiglio was a heavy, big-featured man, casually dressed in some sort of dark, rather nautical-looking sweater, but the Marshal who was no expert in sartorial elegance noticed that the designer's label was prominently displayed on the outside and the shirt and cravat beneath looked like silk.

'This doesn't mean a changing of the guard, I trust?' Robiglio looked from the Marshal to Niccolini. 'You're not leaving us?'

'No, not at all—Marshal Guarnaccia here is just visiting.'

'Really? Any special reason?'

The Marshal sensed Niccolini's hesitation before he said, as the Marshal himself had said: 'There might be and there might not . . .' Niccolini, he decided, didn't like this man.

Signora Tozzi returned with coffee, an unlabelled bottle and three glasses.

'I won't, since I haven't eaten.' Robiglio himself filled their glasses for them. 'I was hoping I'd run into you. When I didn't see you next door I was going to call in at the Station after lunch. I've been thinking it over and I've decided we can take Sestini's boy on.'

'Well, that is good news! Fine. I'll let Sestini know right away. You won't regret it, he's a good lad.'

'I never had any doubts about that. Anyone recommended by you I know I can take without qualms.'

'So you do need another apprentice after all.'

'To be absolutely frank I don't. But I'll fit him in somewhere, have no fear.'

'That's very generous of you.'

'Let's say I can afford to be generous once in a while. In a small town like this a concern as big as mine . . . it's a question of responsibilities . . . Let me fill your glasses. This grappa is something special in my experience. Of course, one can't be generous all the time, it wouldn't be in anyone's interest. If I went out of business it would be a disaster for this area.' He said this with an ingratiating smile aimed at Guarnaccia.

The Marshal watched the two of them in silence, taking in not so much their words, positive and amicable, as the tone of their voices, Robiglio's aggressive charm, Niccolini's closed expression. He continued to stare at them as the conversation drifted to names, families and businesses the

Marshal had never heard of. Was Robiglio really a millionaire as Berti had said when he turned his car at the gates of
the big house with the seven lavatories? Or was it just an
exaggeration? He saw that Niccolini was becoming restless,
as if he wanted to jump up and walk out. He kept up a
stream of cheerful remarks but they became more and more
brief and irrelevant until suddenly he got to his feet when
Robiglio was in the middle of a sentence.

'Right. Fine. Guarnaccia, we must be off and then Signor
Robiglio can settle in where he is and have his lunch.'

'The bill . . .' suggested the Marshal.

'Another time, another time. Nice to have seen you.
Thanks again for fixing up the lad. All the best.' And he
strode from the room without even waiting to see whether
the Marshal was following him.

His farewell to the Tozzis was almost as brusque, and
only when they were out of the restaurant did he change to
a lower gear and say: 'Sorry about that, Guarnaccia. Maybe
you wanted another coffee.'

'No matter.'

'I can't do with that man. Can't do with him at all.'

'So I noticed.'

'You did?' Niccolini looked astonished. 'I'm not one to
quarrel with anybody, why should I bother? In a town as
small as this one . . . and he's a big noise around here.'

'So he said.'

'I like to keep my opinions to myself. I have to. You don't
think he noticed anything, do you?'

'Perhaps not . . .' The Marshal thought Robiglio would
have had to be blind and deaf not to have noticed Niccolini's
antipathy but he didn't like to say so. Niccolini seemed
convinced of his own subtlety.

'Well, it's no skin off my nose.'

'No.'

'Thing is to be on friendly terms with everybody, but
what the hell—you're sure he noticed nothing?'

'Well . . .'

'No, no! Thing is to be polite. You're probably one of those people who notices things.'

'Yes.'

They crossed a bridge with its low railings painted bright yellow and were back in the town square flanked by the Carabinieri Station, a church, a couple of bars and some shops with their metal shutters rolled down. In the centre of the square stood the dripping bronze figure of a partisan baring his chest in defiance at the enemy. It was true that the rain had stopped but the pavements were still wet and dirty and the puddles full. The air was as cold and damp as ever, the square more or less deserted at this hour. Above the bars and shops the soaked yellow stucco was peeling and broken around the brown shutters of the apartments. Wet weather seemed to be the town's natural element. It was impossible to imagine the place in full sunlight.

'I suppose the town used to consist of just this area here,' the Marshal said as they strolled across the square, avoiding the bigger puddles. He said it more to distract Niccolini from his worries than out of any genuine interest. The place depressed him.

'That's right, before they built the factories, the post-war ones, that is. There was just the old centre here and the Medici Villa—that's up there on the hill but in this weather you can barely see it.'

A milky mist filled the valley and covered the lower part of the hill. Where it stopped the black shapes of a row of cypresses and umbrella pines apparently suspended in mid-air were silhouetted against the grey sky, indicating the hill's summit. Of the villa the Marshal could make out nothing.

'If it were a fine day, now . . .' Niccolini dismissed the villa with a wave of his hand. 'Let's have a coffee in the bar! What time do you want to get back?'

'I'll take the first bus that comes along.'

'We'll ask inside. Never use the bus myself so I don't know the timetable. Ah! Two coffees, if you please, and a bus to Florence for the Marshal here if you can lay that on, too!'

'There's one in about a quarter of an hour. We've got tickets if you need one.'

The poorly lit bar was empty except for a boy playing a pinball machine at the back.

'He's intending to get himself elected, that's what it is,' said Niccolini, banging his cup down on the saucer.

'Robiglio? At the municipal elections?'

'And I can tell you that I've taken advantage of the fact to help a few people out.'

'Why not?'

'But I'll tell you something else. He refused to take the Sestini lad on last week—well, he wouldn't get their vote if he were the only one standing, they're staunch communists, so I didn't have high hopes but I thought I'd try anyway . . . Sestini's a good worker, mould-maker at Moretti's place, but of course Moretti already has an apprentice so in a place that small he couldn't take the son on even to oblige a good worker. And now our friend Robiglio's changed his mind, you notice?'

'About taking the lad on? Yes.'

'I wonder why.'

'Well, you know him better than I do. I couldn't say.'

'I know him all right. There's a lot in his past, as I've heard it, that wouldn't bear much scrutiny.'

'How long ago in the past?'

'During the war. I don't know the full story but I've heard things. A blackshirt who managed to survive the aftermath, you know the sort I mean. His father was mayor here under Mussolini. Of course with the money and influential friends they had it wasn't long before they came to the top of the pile again once the fuss died down.'

'I see. You think he's frightened of something?'

'It's a long time ago but people don't forget.'

'You're sure it's not likely to be something more recent? After all, last week he wouldn't help you—and I got the impression, to tell you the truth, that he wasn't too pleased about my being here.'

'D'you think so? I said you were one of those people who notice things! Well, I don't like it.'

'I can see that. If it's of any interest, he saw me leaving Moretti's place.'

'He did? Well, I can't see him having anything to do with small fry like Moretti . . . Anyway, I shall keep an eye on him.'

'It might be an idea. I think I'd better be on my way.'

In fact, the bus was already pulling into the square and the Marshal only just had time to jump on followed by Niccolini's 'All the best, all the best! We'll be in touch . . .'

He almost, but not quite, fell asleep on the bus, and when his wife greeted him by saying, 'Since you've been out all day and probably haven't eaten properly I've cooked something a bit special for supper . . .' she looked so put out at his groan of dismay that he told her all about his day at the potteries and about Niccolini.

'He sounds quite a character.'

'He is.'

'Will you be going back there? Was it something important?'

For he hadn't told her the reason.

'I don't know yet. Maybe not.'

But he wasn't convinced. And so he wasn't surprised when first thing next morning he received a telephone call. Niccolini was as noisy and bursting with life as ever but there was that same note of strain in his voice as there had been in the presence of Robiglio.

'It's about that lass!'

'The Swiss girl?'

'That's right. She's been found.'

'Then she was out there.'

'She was here all right. Under a sherd ruck.'

'What's that? I don't follow you . . .'

'Local man found her. He was crossing the field behind

Moretti's place to go pruning and when he passed the sherd ruck he saw some hair . . . Like as not she'd been buried completely but the ruck shifts every so often, you know what I mean.'

'I don't—'

'I've got to get back there right away. Magistrate's waiting. I'll have to leave you.'

And he rang off.

CHAPTER 3

No sooner had the Marshal replaced the receiver than the phone rang again:

'Guarnaccia? Maestrangelo.'

'Good morning, Captain.'

'I have something for you about that missing Swiss girl.'

The Marshal listened without interrupting to say he already knew; he let the Captain finish and then only asked him:

'Are you going out there?'

'I'm about to leave now with the substitute prosecutor, after which I can leave things in Niccolini's hands since I'm snowed under here. I take it you can handle the case from this end, get me some information on the girl, home address, friends and contacts in Florence and so on? Given that she lives in your quarter.'

'Of course.'

'Good. Then, if you haven't got too heavy a day, you might want to come with us, given that you're going to collaborate. Did you go out and see Niccolini yesterday?'

'Yes. Yes, I did.'

'He seems competent enough, though it bothers me somewhat that he's only been here a year or so . . .'

So what did he expect from someone who's only been there once? There were times when his captain's faith in him troubled the Marshal. It was true that once or twice in the past he'd made himself useful, but only when all that had been required was simple observation. He hadn't the brains or the training for anything beyond that. Besides which, Niccolini might welcome cooperation but not interference. Captain Maestrangelo was always scrupulously polite and correct but the Marshal guessed from his tone of voice that he was about to start putting pressure on him and when that happened the Marshal became as immovable as solid rock.

'To tell you the truth,' he began slowly, 'I've got an appointment in half an hour with Dr Biondini here at the Palatine Gallery . . . Some security headaches over this new exhibition. In fact, I wanted to have a word with you about it. I'm afraid I'll have to ask you for an extra man—'

'I'll send you somebody. No problem.'

'Unless we're hit by the first wave of 'flu in the meantime.'

'You'll have the men you need.'

'Even so, I can hardly break this appointment, time being so short.'

The last thing he wanted was to spend the morning in the company of a substitute prosecutor who would resent the presence of an NCO and address himself exclusively to the Captain, who would in turn insist on including his Marshal as he had done in the past. It was embarrassing. It made a man feel ridiculous. And now the Captain was annoyed. His tone became a shade more brusque.

'In that case perhaps you could find time to see Niccolini later this morning and organize things between you.'

This time it was an order.

'Yes, sir.'

Well, he was annoyed himself. It was one thing asking him to collaborate from this end, all very proper, but he knew from past experience that the Captain expected more of him than that. Where was the sense of it? Those people out there didn't like outsiders. If they wouldn't talk to Niccolini they surely wouldn't talk to him.

He was still annoyed when he came back from his appointment with Biondini and went through to his quarters to get a cup of coffee before leaving.

'Go and sit in the other room and I'll bring it to you.' His wife was washing the kitchen floor and the chairs were stacked upside down on the table so that there was no place for him.

He went into the living-room but instead of sitting down he walked about unhappily as if he were in somebody else's house and had no business . . . well, he wasn't going to interfere. Collaborate from this end was what he would do and no more.

'Here you are. Why don't you sit down for a minute?'

'I haven't time.' He took the cup and drank off the coffee in one go.

The truth was he would willingly have sat down for five minutes now he thought about it, time to recover his temper, but at that moment his wife produced a vacuum-cleaner and started pushing the furniture about.

'Couldn't you do that later?'

'But you said you were going out . . .'

The telephone rang.

'Is it for me?'

'No.' And his wife began an incomprehensible conversation, evidently something or other to do with the school their two boys attended, probably another parent. He would have liked to talk to her for a minute, not that she could help, just to get it off his chest. But the conversation went on and on.

'No, no . . . you're right, absolutely right, and if we wait until the next parent-teachers meeting . . . She did? And what did he say? No . . . No, it isn't. Well the distance wouldn't be a problem if—exactly. Exactly!'

In the end the Marshal stepped over the vacuum-cleaner and stumped out of the room, leaving the door open.

The hill of broken pottery looked as though it were steaming in the watery sunlight that was breaking through the mist.

From where he stood at a distance the Marshal could see men climbing over it, moving slowly and with difficulty, sometimes going down on all fours. They must have been trying their best not to disturb anything but every now and then the sherd ruck would cave in under them, upsetting their balance and sending a flurry of potsherds rattling down the side of the heap. A man in civilian clothing, no doubt a magistrate, was talking vehemently to Niccolini, sometimes pointing across the glistening wet field beyond the sherd ruck to where the town was shrouded in thick mist below the line of dark cypress and the faint outline of the villa, sometimes at the ramshackle factory where the chimney was smoking fiercely and radiating waves of heat that were visible in the cold air. The Marshal stood very still, watching it all from behind his dark glasses, his hands buried deeply in the pockets of his black greatcoat. He was too far away to hear anything the magistrate was saying but after a moment he heard a shout and one of the men scrambling on the ruck held something up. Niccolini and the magistrate dropped their conversation and went over to examine the find. Where they had been standing a shrouded white form became visible on the ground. After a moment, Niccolini returned and stood looking down at it, rubbing a big hand over his face. Then he looked up and spotted the Marshal and raised his hand in salute. He came tramping across the wet field, his cheeks red and his eyes bright in the cold sunshine.

'Good morning, good morning! A bad business, this. A bad business altogether. Well, we've found your missing girl for you. It remains to be seen whether we find whoever did away with her. That might not be so easy. Well, some saint or other will help us out.'

'Let's hope so.' What had the Captain said to him? Was Niccolini, though as hearty in his greeting as ever, a little embarrassed? The Marshal had no intention of interfering unnecessarily, but he couldn't help being intrigued. His glance shifted to the right and the shimmering heat around the black chimney.

'Is it his, all this?'

'Moretti's? No, no. All the land around here belongs to Robiglio's estate. Moretti rents this field off him including where the factory stands. The orchards over there belong to the chap who found the body. He was going over there to do some pruning. The sherd ruck's Moretti's, of course, although any number of people make use of it to dump anything they want to get rid of.'

'Including our friend Berti?'

'No, Berti no. Though he fires here so anything of his that's spoilt or broken gets dumped here.'

They were silent for a while, watching the men who continued to search the sherd ruck.

'No sightseers,' the Marshal observed.

'I cleared them off first thing. I must say I wasn't expecting this. Wherever that lass might have finished up I wouldn't have thought . . . I've never had anything serious since I've been here bar one or two burglaries, never anything like this. Well, there it is. I'm sorry, very sorry. Well!' He clapped his big hands together. 'We'd better make a start. I gather you're going to be helping us.'

He was smiling broadly but wasn't there that same note of strained enthusiasm which the Marshal had noted in his dealings with Robiglio? Guarnaccia's troubled eyes avoided those of his colleague.

'I'll do what I can from my end. At least I can get some information on the girl for you from her flatmate, the school she used to attend and so on—'

'What? No! The way I understood it, you were to give me a hand here. On the spot! Don't tell me you can't spare me a bit of time. Come on now, nobody's as indispensable as all that. I'm counting on you.' His irritation was unmistakable but he was determined to be cheerful and make the best of a bad job. He even went so far as to slap the Marshal heartily on the back.

'Let's be going. You'd better take a look at the lass, though it's not a pretty sight.'

And the Marshal suffered himself to be taken off in the direction of the sherd ruck, forcing himself to keep up with Niccolini's great plunging strides but too busy with his own preoccupations to bother following the inevitable monologue until he realized it was touching on himself.

'We heard about that in Rome even. Of course, an international crook of that calibre, everybody knew, though I didn't realize at the time that you were the one who got him for doing in that German woman.'

'I didn't get him,' pointed out Guarnaccia, disturbed by such garbled tales going about. 'He died—'

'Here we are . . .' Only one young man in uniform stood guard beside the shrouded form by this time.

'You can go, lad. We'll stay until the ambulance comes.'

'It's already arrived. They're parked in front of the factory since they can't get any nearer and will have to bring the stretcher for her. The magistrate's gone now to say they can take her.'

'Get along, then. Go back in the van with the others.'

'What about you?'

'Marshal Guarnaccia here will give me a lift—you're in your car today?'

The Marshal nodded and the young man left them, touching his cap in salute and walking around the canvas sheet at a good distance without looking down. Probably he had managed to avoid looking at the body the whole time he'd been there.

'National Service?' the Marshal guessed.

'That's right. And you can bet your life his mother'll be on the phone to me before long, wanting me to keep him out of this lot. Comes from a good family, you know the sort of thing—wanted forty-eight hours' leave a couple of months ago to ride his horse in the Four Year Old Trials at Grosseto, and he got it, too, since they know all the right people. Take a look . . .'

Niccolini had lifted the sheet as he spoke.

'That cut . . .' began the Marshal, frowning.

'It looks odd, I know, but that's because it happened after she died, probably caused by a sharp piece of broken pottery when she was dumped here.'

'There's no doubt that she didn't die here?'

'None. And what's more she wasn't dressed when she died, or not fully. She wasn't wearing these jeans, for instance, they were put back on her afterwards, according to the doctor.'

The Marshal looked down in silence at the dark, swollen face. A flap of skin hung down from the gashed cheek and one glazed eye was partly open, giving the impression of an unpleasant leer. Only the blonde hair, wet and dirty though it was, gave an idea of what the girl's appearance had been when alive.

'What a wreckage . . .' Niccolini might have been reading his thoughts. 'If you'd known her . . .' He dropped the sheet abruptly. 'Her underwear's missing.'

Once the stretcher-bearers arrived they turned away and crossed the sodden field in the direction of the factory.

'I'm going to have a word with Moretti,' said Niccolini as they neared the building, one wall of which shimmered with heat. It seemed as though the fierce roar of the kiln inside must burst the whole ramshackle construction. 'He put up a bad show when the Captain and the magistrate were here. Even if he knows nothing, he needs to change his attitude or he'll find himself in trouble.'

'Do you think he really knows nothing?'

'At this point I've honestly no idea—no, that's not strictly true. In my opinion, in a town this small everybody knows something about whatever happens. I'll talk to him anyway.'

'I can wait for you in the car if you want to see him alone,' suggested the Marshal.

'You're to stay with me, no?'

And the Marshal had no choice but to follow reluctantly in his wake as he took the steps two at a time and strode into the factory, making his way towards the source of heat and noise through the labyrinth and grumbling each time he mistook his way: 'What a place!'

When they entered the kiln room the Marshal all but took a step backwards, not so much because of the intense heat which hit him in a sudden wave but at the sight of the kiln itself, which he had last seen gaping and dark and which now seemed alive as it roared and trembled, the flames licking around holes in the bricked-up front as though some dragon inside were trying to fight its way out. There was no sign of Moretti but the big man in the woolly hat was there, bending over to adjust the tap on a gas pipe leading to the fire. Niccolini tapped him on the shoulder and he looked round without straightening up. His face was red and sweat trickled down from his hat which made the Marshal wonder that he didn't take it off.

'Where is he?' bellowed Niccolini.

The man looked up at the high, blackened ceiling and pointed without troubling to try and make himself heard, then indicated with a brief nod the direction they should take.

In the next room a man sat working alone, gouging deep patterns into a red jar that revolved slowly between his knees. His hands and face and clothes were stained with the same rusty tint and his boots were buried in the leathery red ribbons he had cut away, so that he seemed to have been planted there and to have absorbed the predominant colour of his surroundings over the years. He watched them walk by with eyes devoid of expression and with no pause in the rhythmic movements that sent more ribbons of clay spinning on to the pile at his feet.

Niccolini strode past without bestowing a glance on him, but the Marshal met his blank gaze, conscious again of being an intruder and of having no real existence for these people. He would have liked to stop, to insist on making some sort of contact, but the last thing he wanted was to get lost in this maze of a place alone and Niccolini was already into the next room and blustering:

'Looking for Moretti! Where's the staircase?'

The Marshal had no choice but to follow him.

One of the three throwers working side by side at their wheels withdrew a muddy red arm from inside a spinning cylinder to point: 'Through there on your right.'

There was no chance to linger here either but, even so, Guarnaccia's big eyes took in the room at a glance and he murmured as he passed the man who had spoken: 'Who works there?' There was a fourth wheel with a wedge of clay waiting on it.

'Moretti.' The thrower plunged his arm back into the cylinder and bowed his head over it as its sides suddenly bulged and grew at the base.

He caught Niccolini up on the wooden staircase, puffing a little in an effort to keep up with the latter's determined strides.

'What a place,' Niccolini went on grumbling, 'what a shambles . . . Now where are we . . .?'

They paused at the top of the stairs, doubtful as to which way to go next until they heard voices ahead, two voices, one of which suddenly rose above the other in anger.

'And I'm telling you, like I've always told you, you'll not get away with it twice. The girl's dead, for God's sake!'

The other voice made some inaudible reply. The Marshal and Niccolini moved towards the noise, quickening their pace slightly as if conscious of some impending danger.

'What's it got to do with me? The same as it's got to do with anyone in this town who has a daughter! It's bad enough that crazy bitch of a nymphomaniac—'

Niccolini and the Marshal were almost running, stumbling over unexpected steps, brushing against protruding shelves and tables that marked their black greatcoats with red dust, but over the noise of their own heavy footsteps they heard the choked cry and the short scuffle that preceded a crash so violent it made the floor beneath them shake. Then they came into the long bare room above the kiln and saw Moretti and one of his men struggling with each other in silence. Moretti's hands were at the other's throat but it was his own face that was red, as though he were the one being choked.

'That's enough!' bellowed Niccolini.

Moretti's hands dropped slowly to his sides and hung there.

Neither he nor the man looked at the intruders; they continued to stare at each other, breathing heavily.

'What's it all about?' said Niccolini, approaching them. 'Well? Moretti? Sestini?'

The Marshal stayed away from them, watching. Moretti, with his red-stained clothes, disordered red hair and flushed and angry face, looked like a devil popped out of his own kiln. The other man, Sestini, was white all over. He must have been in charge of the strange plaster shells which had so puzzled the Marshal on his first visit. One of these huge shapes lay smashed into three pieces on the floor, and one of the pieces was rocking with a gentle bumping noise.

In the end it was Sestini who spoke, though with his eyes still fixed on Moretti.

'Nothing,' he mumbled, 'just a personal disagreement . . .'

'Disagreement?' thundered Niccolini. 'Good God! Listen, Moretti, I came back to warn you to change your attitude if you don't want to find yourself in trouble with us, and I find you trying to choke one of your best workers—'

'Like I said,' interrupted Sestini, 'a personal matter.' And he turned away, bending to examine the broken plaster shell. 'Blast! I can't do anything with this . . .'

Moretti's colour was returning to normal but his eyes were still fixed on Sestini, following every move he made. The Marshal, from his position near the door, was pretty sure that the expression in them was one of gratitude. The expression on his colleague's face was of someone about to lose his temper. He was almost as red as Moretti had been.

'Listen!' he began again.

'No, you listen to me,' shouted Moretti, suddenly turning on him, 'I've had enough for one day! People nosing around the place, interrupting the work, asking stupid questions— whatever happened to that girl is no responsibility of mine. What happens to people is more often than not their own fault!'

'Their own fault!' roared Niccolini, towering over the smaller man as though he would have liked to pick him up and shake him. 'Did you see the state of that girl's body? Well? Did you?'

'It's no responsibility of mine!' insisted Moretti, running a hand roughly through his hair and glancing about him as if in search of some concrete proof to offer for his statement.

The Marshal came forward and asked quietly: 'Nympho-maniac, was she? Isn't that what somebody was saying?'

Moretti looked taken aback, either by this remark or because he had been unaware of the Marshal's presence until then.

'Nobody said that . . .'

'Oh no?' Niccolini looked from Moretti to the Marshal and back again. 'Well then, Marshal Guarnaccia and I must be getting hard of hearing. Both of us.'

'Or you've got it in for me, like everybody else around here.'

'Nobody's got it in for you to my knowledge, have they to your knowledge, Guarnaccia?'

The Marshal remained silent. Heat was coming up through the floorboards in suffocating waves and he would have liked to take off his greatcoat. He tucked his hat under his arm and fished for a handkerchief to wipe his brow.

'Well, let's hear it?' Moretti was almost bowed over backwards by Niccolini's aggressiveness.

'I . . .'

'Well? For instance?'

'I didn't mean anything by it,' mumbled Moretti, 'I just lost my temper—and so might you if you were in my position.'

'If I were in your position I'd be a damn sight more careful about losing my temper. Now, you listen to me: if you had nothing to do with this business you've nothing serious to worry about, but don't go putting people's backs up. Keep your head and give a straight answer to a straight question, not like this morning. No good can come of that sort of behaviour. You've got a cast-iron alibi and so have all your men since they were all of them at Tozzi's—but start trying to be clever with us and we're going to start thinking that one way or another you had something to do with that girl's death. Do I make myself clear?'

'I had nothing to do with it.'

'Then stop trying to pull the wool over my eyes! What were you two fighting about just now?'

'Like he said, it was a personal matter, something between us two and nothing to do with the girl. I've never harmed a soul in my life, anybody in this town can tell you that.'

'I don't doubt they could, but unfortunately nobody in this town is likely to tell me anything. They're all like you. And you'd do well to remember on that score that the people in charge of this investigation don't know you or anything about you. All they know is that the girl's body was found on your sherd ruck—and then I find you with your hands at Sestini's throat—Stop that blasted row, can't you?'

Sestini had rolled the broken shells of plaster into a corner and was breaking them into smaller bits with a mallet. He stopped what he was doing without comment and began dropping the pieces into a black polythene rubbish bag. The Marshal left Niccolini to his fruitless attempt at reasoning with Moretti and walked over to him.

'What are those things, anyway?'

'Moulds.'

'They're a funny shape.'

'They're in two parts, sometimes three. Have to be bound together with wire. This one's had it, that's for sure . . .'

'Does he often get that violent?'

Sestini shrugged without answering and the Marshal gave

it up. He didn't see how anybody would ever get to the bottom of this business if guilty and innocent alike remained silent, and it looked as though that was how it was going to be.

He stood looking out of the broken window where the rain had been blowing through the day before. The busy road, having swept away in a big curve from the railway and its high black wall, was slightly less dreary here than outside Berti's place, but not much. No doubt this had been a pleasant enough country area when the big house across the way had been built.

The house of the seven lavatories . . .

Niccolini's voice was rising in exasperation again but the Marshal was unaware of what he was saying. It had occurred to him that there was one person in the town who did talk, and incessantly at that. Robiglio, unpleasant though he was, didn't belong to the rest of them. He didn't have the stubborn peasant mentality that maintained an obstinate silence against all the odds, not trusting himself to speak nor anyone else to believe him if he did. A sophisticated man, a man of the world, Signor Robiglio. He might lie through his back teeth but he'd say something. The yellow façade of the big house was beginning to dry in patches in the pale sunshine. Probably it never got thoroughly dry before the rain began again in this Godforsaken place . . . except perhaps in midsummer when Robiglio was no doubt away. He was the sort who'd have a house in some fashionable seaside resort, or even abroad.

The tall windows returned his gaze blankly.

Sestini had begun hammering again and this time nobody told him to stop. The Marshal glanced over his shoulder. Niccolini had a big hand on Moretti's shoulder and was talking in a lower, more urgent voice, but Moretti wouldn't meet his eyes. Where was the use of it? He would go his own way, for good or evil, as people always did who had been brought up to trust nobody outside their own families. With a sigh, the Marshal turned back to the window. Then he took a step forward and peered out more intently. The tall windows were no longer all blank. Someone was staring out over there as he was staring out here. Were they staring at each other? The house of the seven lavatories, being set well back from the road with its drive leading in from the high gates, was too far away to tell. The Marshal didn't move away. In any case, his car was parked outside advertising his presence. There was no telling who the person across the way was. It might well not be Robiglio himself, who would surely be at his factory at that hour, but even so, that pale blur served to confirm the impression that Robiglio was disturbed for some reason by the Marshal's presence, disturbed enough to make him take on an apprentice he didn't need. And if he remembered correctly . . . Sestini had tied up the rubbish bags and was stacking them against the wall.

'Isn't it your son who's going to be taken on at Robiglio's?'

'What of it?'

The Marshal just stared at him. There was no point in wasting his breath. You couldn't arrest the entire population of the town for reticence.

Perhaps the same thought had crossed Niccolini's mind.

'You'll end up inside, you mark my words! I advise you to think over what I've said because if you do end up inside you'll find it anything but easy to get out again. Well, answer me! Or am I talking to the wall? Ye gods!'

And without a word of warning he turned and strode out of the room, forgetting, or choosing to forget, that he hadn't arrived alone. The Marshal mopped his brow again, put on his hat and followed slowly in his wake. And if he got lost again it was too bad. He was in no mood to go chasing after this volcano of a man every time he went steaming off in a temper.

In fact he only got lost once, having got a better idea of the place by now, and luckily he came across the apprentice who was cutting big wedges of clay with a length of wire as it issued in a thick tube from what looked like a giant sausage-machine. The boy gave him directions sensibly enough, though the Marshal couldn't help remembering the childish clay models he had seen on the windowsill the day before and wondering if the lad weren't a little backward.

Niccolini was stamping his boots by the car.

'Cold,' he said, glaring about him, and once in the passenger seat: 'Damp, more than anything.'

The Marshal started the engine and glanced across at the gates of Robiglio's house.

'I was wondering—'

'We'll go to Berti's place if you don't mind,' interrupted Niccolini. 'He knows more about that lass than anybody else round here, and, by God, if he starts being shifty with me I'll have him inside before he knows what's hit him.'

Berti was anything but shifty in his greeting.

'You're back, then, are you? Have you arrested Moretti?'

Niccolini was too taken aback at this opening to be aggressive.

'What do you mean by that?'

'A straight enough question, I would have thought. If that's where the girl was on Monday . . .'

'That's yet to be proved. For all we know she could have been here.'

'She was found at Moretti's, wasn't she? You don't mind if I go on working . . .' He was seated in his usual place near the blocked-out window. 'You're not going to tell me you're looking for something for your wife today, I imagine.'

'You don't seem too put out by what's happened.'

'Life goes on,' said Berti, searching among the pots of colour for the brush he needed, 'life goes on. Nobody knows that better than I do. I can't offer both of you a seat but one of you could sit down.'

The dusty chair was still drawn up where the Marshal had sat.

'We don't want chairs, we want information,' said Niccolini brusquely, 'about the girl.'

'We went through all that with your chief earlier, didn't we?'

'And you had as little to say for yourself as everyone else round here, though you were the one who had most contact with her.'

Berti traced the outline of a flower delicately on to the plate in front of him and put the brush down. He rubbed his spidery fingers together, looking from one to the other of the two men above him, his tiny eyes glinting.

'If you're thinking what I think you're thinking, Niccolini, you're barking up the wrong tree.'

'Oh, am I? I've seen the way you looked at her.'

'The way I look at women never did them any harm. On the contrary, they like it. There was a time—and not that long ago either—when I could take on three in one day.' This last remark he chose for some reason to direct at the Marshal.

'Three in one day . . .' and he made a sudden gesture with his fingers so vulgar that the Marshal involuntarily took a step backwards and all but collided with the door which somebody was trying to open.

'Shut it, shut it,' Berti said, calling out to the invisible intruder: 'Go away, I'm busy.'

'Who's that?' Niccolini whipped round and the Marshal opened the door in time to see a small woman turn away and scuffle back towards the house next door in her slippers.

'It's only Tina,' Berti said, picking up his brush again, 'the woman from next door.'

'The one whose husband found the body? What does she want with you?' Niccolini pushed past the Marshal and strode outside. The woman had vanished. 'Well,' he said, coming back in and towering over the wizened little artisan as though he intended to eat him alive, 'what's she doing coming round here?'

'She's my neighbour, isn't she? Comes round for a chat now and then.' He chuckled quietly to himself and added: 'If you really want to know what she comes for . . .' He put down his brush carefully and turned to a shelf behind him where there was a stack of dusty books on Majolica and some loose pages cut out of magazines of art history from which he no doubt copied motifs. Underneath these were some glossy magazines, one of which he pulled out and waved in their faces. 'She likes to borrow these. Here, take a look.'

The thin grey fingers clutching the large pornographic image made its garish colours look all the more shocking.

'Cut it out, Berti,' barked Niccolini.

'You wanted to know . . .' Berti evidently took great delight in anything he thought might shock them, and the Marshal was convinced that this was particularly directed at him. It was at him that Berti winked now, saying, 'It's a dull enough life round here, so we have to get a bit of excitement where we can find it.'

'I think,' said the Marshal slowly, 'that I might as well have a word with this woman next door . . .'

He had no real reason for doing it except that he was only too glad to escape from Berti and the jumbled studio with its smells of dust and paraffin and from the leering face and the pornographic magazines. Niccolini made no objection. He was probably glad enough to see the back of his colleague, whatever the excuse. Once outside, he paused a moment, feeling the need to breathe clean air. The mist that had veiled the thin sunshine earlier had thickened, and the sky was a uniform pale grey above the high black wall and the wires of the electric railway line. The traffic streamed past him as he stood there on the patch of beaten dirt in front of Berti's door. A dull life . . . And before the day was out it would almost certainly rain again.

Behind him Niccolini's voice was getting louder and he wondered, too, whether his own presence wasn't the real cause of the trouble rather than the uncommunicative townsfolk. In any case there was little he could do about either problem. With a sigh, he turned and knocked on the small door by the barred window. The cat wasn't there today but the smell was as pungent as ever and he wrinkled his nose as he waited. It was a long wait. He had to knock three times before he heard the woman's shuffling steps, and even then they didn't come as far as the door. He wasn't surprised when after a moment he heard a flutter among the scratching hens and found himself peered at from behind the bars. He stared back at the pale face and waited. When it vanished he knocked hard on the door again, just in case she was thinking he might give up and go away, but the shuffling steps came right up to the door which opened just enough for the face to peer out. To his surprise the face wasn't hostile; it showed a childlike curiosity.

'Who are you?'

'Guarnaccia. Marshal of Carabinieri. I'd like to come in and talk to you for a moment.'

'*He* won't like it.'

Despite this remark, the door opened wider and the Marshal removed his hat and stooped slightly to enter. He found himself in a short dark corridor where the smell from the livestock in the room on the left was quite overpowering and he was glad enough to follow the woman through a door on the right and shut it behind him quickly.

'I usually leave it open,' said the woman, who had stopped in the middle of the room and was watching him. 'I like a bit of air. But perhaps you're cold . . .'

'I am,' the Marshal assured her, 'very cold.' It was true enough in any case and he looked hopefully through a whitewashed archway to the kitchen where a stove was roaring comfortably in the gloom with a pan of water steaming on top of it. But the woman stayed where she was in what must have been the sitting-room, though it was very small and windowless and there was little enough to sit on. It was badly lit by an unshaded light bulb. She offered him a hard and very uncomfortable chair and stood over him, watching while he sat down and planted his hat on his knees, looking about him. The only sound was the ticking of a heavy old-fashioned clock. The focal point of the room was a new white washing-machine with a bunch of plastic flowers in a vase on a bit of coloured cloth standing on it and a dismal-looking wedding photograph on the wall above it. The washing-machine was the only acknowledgement of the busy road that had swept through this rural corner to the new industrial zone further on. In every other way the cottage was a poverty-stricken reminder of the Marshal's own childhood. He was aware of the woman's rather foolish gaze fixed on him, waiting for him to speak.

'Your husband's out working?' he asked her at last, glancing at the dismal wedding photograph.

'He's over at the orchard, pruning.'

'Why don't you sit down yourself?' he suggested, a bit disconcerted by her hovering over him, staring like that.

She sat down obediently and pulled a shapeless woollen cardigan around the bib of her flowered apron. 'Cold . . .' She got up again and the Marshal followed suit, assuming that they were going to remove to the kitchen, but she said: 'I'll be back in a minute . . .' and he sat down again. He watched her hook up the plate of the stove and drop a log of wood into it. Then she took a small earthenware pot and filled it with hot ash and cinders from below. This offering she placed on the concrete floor between their two chairs and sat down again, smiling. The little black cat which had peered through the bars at the Marshal the day before appeared from nowhere and settled itself beside the pot, purring loudly.

'It was your husband, wasn't it, who found the body?'

'That's right.'

'He was on his way to work?'

'He was going pruning,' explained the woman patiently, and she began staring at him with such fascinated intensity that he began to think he had a smut on his face, perhaps a streak of clay.

'Is something the matter?' he said at last. Her look became a sly one. She was younger than the Marshal had first thought, and while not exactly cross-eyed there was something slightly out of true about her eyes.

'I only wanted to ask you,' she said, 'if it's true you come from Florence.'

'I wasn't born there, if that's what you mean.' The Marshal was taken aback by this question. 'But I live there.'

'You came all that way today?'

'I . . . yes . . .'

'And did it take a long time?'

'Only half an hour or so, it's not far—you mean you've never been to Florence?'

'No, but I've heard there are big churches there and statues.' She giggled and stared at him again.

'Do you never go out, then?'

'Oh yes. There's a shop down the road that I go to, and I've been to the town, as well. *He* took me.'

'Your husband?'

'That's right. Him.'

The Marshal looked around the room uneasily. Not only was there no window here, there didn't seem to be one in the kitchen either, as far as he could make out. At one time Berti's place must have been part of the cottage and this half had been for beasts and storage. He remembered her face peering through the barred window, then he remembered something else.

'You go next door sometimes, don't you? To see Berti.'

'When he's not busy he lets me go in and talk to him. And he lets me—'

'But it wasn't him, was it,' interrupted the Marshal, hoping to avoid the subject of the magazines which disturbed him more than ever in the face of this poor childlike creature, 'who told you about the churches and statues in Florence?'

'No, no. The signorina told me.'

'Well, that's one mystery solved,' said the Marshal half to himself.

'Is it a mystery? Puss, puss, come here . . .' She picked up the thin black cat and warmed her hands on its hot fur, sliding her slippered feet nearer to the pot of cinders.

'Just a manner of speaking. Berti told me he often turned

up late in the mornings and that the young girl who used
to come and work for him had no key. I couldn't imagine
her just standing out there in the pouring rain.'
    'She did stand in the rain one day and I saw her.'
    'And invited her in?'
    'She used to talk to me. She had pretty hair and now she's
dead. She gave me a present, though. Do you want me to
show you?'
    'If you like.'
    She shuffled into the kitchen and got a cardboard box
down from a shelf. She didn't bring the box with her but
opened it on the kitchen table and took out something flat.
    'Here it is.' She shuffled back, holding out the treasure to
him. 'I keep it in the bag she brought it in.'
    A stationer's paper bag with a postcard inside it showing
a view of the Palazzo della Signoria.
    'You can see the clock on the front of the church, and the
statues, and the people going in.'
    The Marshal decided against trying to explain to her that
it wasn't a church. What was the point? He only said:
    'Perhaps you'll go there one day.'
    She shook her head. 'He won't let me.'
    'And do you always do what he tells you?'
    She chuckled, driving the cat from her chair and sitting
down again. She leaned closer towards him and confided:
    'I have to, you see, when he's there, or else . . . But once
a week when he goes and plays billiards—' she broke off
and glanced at the door as though afraid that *he* might come
in and pounce on her—'I go and see my brother.'
    'You do?'
    'He lets me talk to him.'
    The same phrase she had used of Berti. She may have
been a bit simple but there was no getting away from the
fact that her loneliness in that bare house with nothing but
the ticking of the big clock and the scratching of hens for
company was as real and soul-destroying as it would have
been for anyone else.

'You won't tell *him*?'

'No, no . . .'

'Because if he finds out he'll lock me up. When he gets really mad he says I should be locked up in the villa.'

'The villa?'

'Up there.' She indicated vaguely with a plump hand. 'So you mustn't say anything.'

'I won't say anything. Which day does he go and play billiards?'

'Thursdays. That's today.'

It was difficult to imagine that she managed to keep track of the passing days which must have been all alike to her, but if Thursdays were so important, then perhaps she did keep track after all. It was worth trying.

'When did you last see the signorina who gave you the postcard?'

'Last week. It rained on Friday and I watched out for her because I hadn't heard Berti's car.'

'And on Monday?'

'On Monday, no.'

'No, what?'

'Berti came early, I heard the car.'

'I see. So you didn't look out for her?'

'I heard his car before the bus so I knew she wouldn't be coming to see me.'

'I see . . .' Well, it had been worth a try.

'She didn't go and see Berti either. I don't know where she went. I saw her go off down the road.'

'You did? Which way?'

'That way, towards the town. Maybe she went to see my brother. He lets people talk to him and she likes to talk to people. So do I. So maybe she went to see him.'

'Maybe she did.'

'He's going to get married one day and then if he has a baby I can play with it.'

'That would be nice . . .' The Marshal began to think he might as well be going. He was willing to believe that she really did remember seeing the girl get off the bus and go down the road on Monday, but hers wasn't evidence that would stand up in court, that was certain. He got to his feet stiffly for the close little room was really very cold.

'You're not going away? I like talking to you.'

'Thank you.' She must be about the only person round these parts who did!

'If I had a baby I'd play with it and dress it. I used to have one but it died and now I can't have any more.'

'I'm sorry.'

'They took everything away.'

'I'm sorry. I really have to go now . . .' The Marshal had edged towards the door.

'I'll show you a picture of him if you like. It was a little boy—I've got it in my box . . .' She shuffled quickly back to the kitchen and there was nothing he could do but wait there by the door twirling his hat between his big hands.

'Here . . .' She hurried back to him. 'Look, isn't he lovely?'

It was indeed a beautiful baby with smooth shining cheeks and soft blond hair. One chubby fist was reaching upwards towards a spoonful of the yellowish baby food which the picture, cut very carefully from a magazine, was advertising.

CHAPTER 4

He decided to wait for Niccolini in the car, switching on the engine to warm himself up. He was aware without looking that Tina occasionally appeared behind the bars to see if he was still there. Perhaps she was resentful that he should have parked himself there instead of staying with her, but that couldn't be helped. He kept his eyes fixed on the high black wall. A train thundered past behind it, making the car vibrate, then there was nothing except lorries and a few private cars. Nobody stopped here, none of the drivers even looked up as they went by. He wondered how much business Berti did and with whom, and before having sat here for long he found himself hoping that somebody would stop, or even that he could see the trains that went by, instead of just hearing them. If he felt like that after ten minutes or so of dull waiting what must it be like to be stuck here for a lifetime? It was true that he was used to the bustle of the city. People got used to anything in time. Even so, he was glad enough when Niccolini burst out of the studio, slamming the door behind him and erupting into the Marshal's tiny Fiat 500 which could hardly contain him.

'Enough's enough,' was all he said. 'Let's get something to eat.'

Well, if he didn't feel like volunteering information the Marshal wasn't one to insist on it, though there was little point in their working together, however unwillingly, if this was the way it was going to be. He pulled out and joined the traffic going towards the town, keeping his own counsel. If he judged his man right, Niccolini would be incapable of remaining silent for more than a few minutes.

It turned out to be a matter of seconds.

'You never know where you are with that chap!'

'No.'

'I'm a simple character myself and I like things to be clear, blast it.'

The Marshal, who felt Niccolini to be a good deal less simple than he appeared or thought himself, made no comment.

'Starts off with "Have you arrested Moretti?" and then defends the fellow's character like he was his greatest friend! Cool as a cucumber, too, though he's not out of the wood himself by any means. No proof that she didn't go to him on Monday, no proof at all.'

'The woman next door—'

'The woman next door—what's she called? Tina—isn't right in the head according to our friend Berti, and that's not all . . .'

He didn't go on.

'You were able to find out something, then?'

'Enough to be going on with.' And he began drumming on the dashboard with a huge gloved hand.

The Marshal could hardly blame him, after all, since he would have strongly resented a total stranger being foisted on him on his own ground. The only thing was to be patient and perhaps to have a word with the Captain and get himself out of all this.

'I thought you might like to know,' he said cautiously, 'that the girl used to take shelter in Tina's house in the mornings when she arrived before Berti and found herself locked out. It's true the woman's not as she should be, of course . . . but though I'm no expert I'd say she had a child's mentality rather than an adult's, which doesn't prevent her from noticing things . . .'

'Noticing things! Noticing what? Probably romancing.'

'She may be . . .' There was no getting away from the baby in the advert. 'But leading the life she does, shut in that house all day . . .'

'She needs to be shut in, by all accounts!'

'By Berti's account,' persisted the Marshal gently. 'And he might have been exaggerating, knowing as he did that I'd gone next door. According to her, she saw the girl on Monday morning get off the bus and go off down the road, and she says Berti was already in his studio by then.'

'Then Berti would have seen her himself. The bus stop's right opposite. What had he to gain by being ambiguous if he saw her go off to Moretti's place? No, no . . .'

'You said yourself,' pointed out the Marshal, 'that he's ambiguous about Moretti, almost accusing him and then defending him.'

'Even so, damn it, if he saw her . . .'

'I don't think it makes all that much difference if he saw her or not.'

'Eh? What does that mean?'

'Well, she went to Berti every day, so if one day she gets

off the bus and goes to Moretti's without bothering to cross the road and tell him so, even though his car's there . . .'

'He'd have known already, of course. Obviously, Moretti was getting ready to fire and Berti was going to take his stuff there so he'd be the one . . .'

'To tell her she could go there.'

'He'd have told her Friday. It's obvious.'

'I expect you're right.'

'Of course I'm right. But he should have told us! I can't do with people who waste my time.'

'Can I park here?'

'Fine, fine. Man must think I was born yesterday.'

The Marshal parked the car.

The wave of heat and good smells of roasting meat which greeted them as they pushed open the glass door was as welcome and comforting as it had been the day before, but the Marshal had a feeling that the noise of conversation in the big dining-room was louder and more agitated than he remembered it. Whether that was true or not, there was no doubt that on Niccolini's first loud "How do you you?" it dropped suddenly and petered away into nothing within seconds, leaving his greeting hanging in the air. A colour television set at the end of the room was giving out the lunch-time news. The Marshal hadn't noticed it on his first visit though it was probably on every day, but now the newscaster's voice was clearly audible above the sound of cutlery and the crackle of the kitchen fire.

Tozzi came hurrying towards them between the rows of tables with their chequered cloths, an anxious smile fixed on his face.

'There's a table coming free in a minute or so next door if you . . .'

'Don't bother,' Niccolini interrupted, 'we'll be fine here at my usual place.' And he sat himself down facing the television.

The Marshal sat down opposite him, aware that every pair of eyes in the big room was fixed on them. Tozzi went

off and didn't come back. A small boy in a white apron
which was much too big for him came to take their order,
and little by little the conversation around them was
resumed, but in subdued tones. The newscaster could still
be heard and the Marshal turned and stared at the scenes
from some foreign war without following what was going
on. When they were served Niccolini ate a dish of spaghetti
with a show of appetite and enthusiasm, but the Marshal
knew he was upset. It must have been the first time he had
walked into that room without almost everyone in it greeting
him cheerily. And the Marshal was willing to bet it was also
the first time that he hadn't gone straight to the kitchen to
lift the lids of the big pans to see what good things were
cooking and then warm himself at the fire, chattering to
everyone around him. His own feeling of annoyance gave
way to one of distress on behalf of this once-cheerful giant
of a man who found himself all of a sudden in a situation
he couldn't cope with. Coming as he did from a very small
town in Sicily, the Marshal was familiar enough with these
sullen silences which often had little or no personal ill-will
in them and which, once past, were forgotten as if they'd
never happened. But Niccolini was a city man, a Roman,
who had probably never encountered such united hostility
in his life, and his character being so exuberant and sociable,
he was bound to take it all the harder. On top of which he
was probably wishing that at least he had one of his own
men with him, perhaps the young brigadier he had mentioned with whom he usually ate, instead of a stranger who
had been planted on him against his will.

The Marshal watched him sympathetically but Niccolini
avoided his eyes. He was affecting to hum a tune to himself
and studying the menu intensely as though he had never
eaten here before and didn't know the dishes of each day by
heart. The best thing would be to say something, start up
a conversation which would at least fill the silence at their
table, but try as he might the Marshal couldn't think of
anything to say. The arrival of their second course was a

welcome distraction, but it would have been so much better if Tozzi had served them himself and passed a word or two with them. There wasn't much hope of starting up a conversation with this fourteen-year-old boy with thin red hands and the enormous apron, and all the Marshal got out was a mumbled 'Thank you'.

Then a group of Moretti's workmen came in and once again the noise level dropped perceptibly. They took the only free table which was just inside the door, so that they never came into Niccolini's line of vision. Nevertheless, he noticed the change of atmosphere and followed the Marshal's glance.

'Who is it?'

'Moretti's men.'

'Anybody speak to them?'

'Not at first, but one of them's just turned round to talk to somebody at the next table. They look to be arguing, though . . .'

'Hear anything of what they're saying?'

'Nothing.' The general conversation had resumed, and with that, the television and the noise from the kitchen it was impossible to pick up a word from so far away.

'Moretti's not with them,' the Marshal added.

'Never is. He and his brother eat at home, except when Moretti brings a customer here. Are they still arguing?'

'Yes. It's one of the throwers, I don't know his name . . .'

By this time the thrower was well aware of the Marshal's watching him and he deliberately raised his voice to make himself heard, though still talking to the same man at the next table.

The Marshal couldn't make the remark out, even so; all he heard clearly was the word 'foreigner' spoken in a tone of loud disgust. He could guess the import well enough, that everybody's life was being disturbed by some foreigner having got herself killed, someone who had nothing to do with them and so didn't count. It fitted in well enough with their general attitude to outsiders.

'Have some of this spinach,' said Niccolini suddenly, reaching over with a loaded spoon.

The Marshal opened his mouth to protest that he wasn't at all fond of spinach, but realized in time that if Niccolini had begun feeding him again the spoonful of bitter greens was worth more than its face value.

'Thanks.'

A trolley with a huge bowlful of *tagliatelli* on it rolled past the Marshal and stopped. Tozzi stood looking down at them.

'Everything to your satisfaction, gentlemen?'

'Fine, fine,' Niccolini answered.

'A bad business, this, about the girl.'

'That's right,' said Niccolini, 'a bad business.'

'Bad for everybody. In a small place like this . . . You mustn't mind the lads being a bit restive . . .'

'I mustn't?'

'What I mean is, there's no cause to take it personally. People round here have a tendency to stick together and bury their differences when there's trouble from . . .'

'From outsiders?'

'You know how it is.'

'I'm beginning to.'

'It was the same during the war.'

'This isn't a war. An innocent girl got herself brutally murdered and nobody in this town gives a damn as far as I can make out!'

'That's not necessarily true. Nobody wants trouble, that's all.'

'Well, they've got it. And what's more they'll go on having it until I put that murderer away. If you like, you can tell them that from me because I reckon that every one of Moretti's men knows who killed that girl as sure as they know they're going to eat that pasta—and maybe you'd better serve it to them before it goes cold.'

'Look, if I've spoken out of turn I beg your pardon. It's just that I know these men and you haven't been here long enough to understand . . . In short, I was trying to be helpful.'

'If you want to be helpful you just give them that message from me . . . and maybe bring us a sweet since we've finished here.'

'I'll send the boy.'

As Tozzi pushed his trolley towards Moretti's men Niccolini met the Marshal's big expressionless eyes.

'You don't need to tell me. I shouldn't have been so sharp with him.'

The Marshal said nothing.

'It's true, we seem to have made enough enemies as it is without creating more ill-feeling. I can see you disapprove.'

The Marshal said nothing.

'I just can't do with the way these people think they can make a fool of me.'

'As far as that's concerned,' said the Marshal slowly, 'I'm inclined to agree with Tozzi. I don't think you should take it so personally.'

'Oh, all right, I know it's not me as a person. If you like it's my uniform they're ignoring. Let's say I'm taking it personally on behalf of the army.'

'Well, I wouldn't bother.' The Marshal remained placid. 'I think the army will survive it.'

Niccolini's face broke into a grin. 'You're right! Why should I bother?' He laughed. 'What a fool I am! Every time I lose my temper I look at myself in the mirror and say, "Niccolini, you're a damn fool! Why should you bother?" I should be more like you and take things calmly. I bet it takes a lot to make you lose your temper. No, no, you're right. We'll take things calmly. Sooner or later we're bound to find out who's responsible for this business.'

'If it comes to that,' the Marshal said, 'I'd be happier if we found out sooner rather than later.' He was looking past Niccolini to where Moretti's men were eating.

'You don't think . . .'

'That they'd take the law into their own hands? Yes, I

do. I think it's just a question of time and that they're working themselves up to it. It's been at the back of my mind since this morning when we interrupted that fight between Moretti and Sestini, but it struck me even more just now when Tozzi mentioned the war. I imagine there were a good few scores settled on the quiet here once the fascists were out.'

'No doubt, no doubt. But then that happened everywhere.'

'Yes. But in the cities it was often a case of lining anybody in a black shirt up against a wall, regardless. In the villages it was a bit different, more personal and a lot less hysterical. You see what I mean?'

'Well, I do . . . but no! The climate was different then. In all that chaos people could get away with anything and they did. No, no. I see what you mean—that may be the way feeling runs, but let's not exaggerate. They can't imagine they'd get away with anything like that now.'

'I hope you're right.'

'So do I hope I'm right. But whether I am or not, if that's the way they're feeling nobody's going to tell us anything helpful.'

'They will. We don't know who yet but they won't all be in agreement and they've probably all got wives . . .'

'Now that's an idea. We could question their wives.'

'No, no,' said the Marshal. 'We won't need to do that. That's not the way of it at all.'

'I know what it is, Guarnaccia: you must come from a place as small as this yourself.'

'Smaller. And I'll be surprised if you don't reap a fine crop of anonymous letters tomorrow morning.'

'Good God! Well, you never cease to learn in this life is what I always say—ah! Let's have a bit of something sweet!'

The boy in the big apron had brought the sweet trolley towards them and stood waiting for their order. Niccolini rubbed his hands together, quite his old self.

'I'd say two good helpings of that chocolate cake, what

about it, Guarnaccia? And don't stint, laddie. Engine can't run without petrol and we have work to do.'

They took their time eating it, and with every intention of lingering over coffee, too.

'Once I get back to the Station,' explained Niccolini, 'there'll be a dozen interruptions, especially as I've been out all morning. When Moretti's men have gone I've got a few things I want to talk over with you.'

The men weren't long in leaving but they didn't go without creating another little scene. Having finished their meal, each of them happened to go to the washroom at the end of the dining-room, and to do so they naturally had to pass by the table where Niccolini was sitting with the Marshal. None of them spoke and one or two of them even went so far as to look quite pointedly at the two uniformed men as if to emphasize that their not speaking was a deliberate act. The last of them to return from the washroom was the thrower who'd begun the argument with a neighbouring table earlier on.

This man passed by the Marshal and Niccolini without a glance but then stopped at a table almost opposite, raising his voice to make sure they could hear him, and spoke to a workman who was sitting there alone with a coffee and a newspaper in front of him.

'Well, and what do you think of this mess? What I say is that it doesn't do to have anything to do with foreigners. I've no time for them myself. Am I right or am I right?'

The man, who had the electricity company's badge on his overalls, looked up, surprised. Then he glanced across the way and realized whom it was aimed at.

'You're right enough,' he said, 'you have to be careful about mixing yourself up with foreigners . . . especially Germans.' And he went back to his newspaper.

The other looked furious but went off without another word.

'Now, what was all that about?' Niccolini frowned. 'I'd have thought everybody knew she was Swiss.'

'Things get garbled,' the Marshal reminded him, 'and she did speak German, so people would notice her accent. Who is that chap, anyway?'

'A cousin of Moretti's.'

'Then we know where he stands. Nothing to hope for there.'

'Nothing. He didn't like the answer he got, though, did he? I can't think why, can you?'

'No.'

'I suppose you're right about the girl's accent . . .'

'I noticed it in her friend. It was thick enough, though her Italian was good. I'd better go back to Florence shortly and have a word with her. Somebody has to tell her what's happened and maybe I can find out a bit more . . . though to tell you the truth she's not much more communicative than this lot here.'

'That's a big help. Well, if ever we needed some saint or other on our side it's now—and all we've got is Berti.'

'He did tell you something, then?'

'He told me one thing, the minute you'd gone next door. Do you know who that woman is? The crazy one?'

'Tina?'

'That's right. Listen to this—I wouldn't have believed it but he can hardly have made it up. She's Moretti's sister.'

'She is?'

'Older sister. How about that for a turn-up for the books? I knew nothing about it, I can tell you—but then it seems he has nothing to do with her, married her off to that peasant farmer who keeps her practically locked up since she's not right in the head.'

'Maybe she's not right in the head because he keeps her locked up,' suggested the Marshal, remembering the silent, smelly house without windows. 'After all, he'd hardly have married her—'

'Wait, I'm coming to that. You didn't see her husband?'

'No, he was out pruning.'

'Right. Pruning his orchards and that's what he married

her for, that land. He's a good twenty years older than she is and a bit of a strange character on his own account. He farms a few acres on the old peasant basis of fifty per cent of the produce and for someone in that position to get their hands on a few acres of their own—well, I don't need to tell you that if you're from a country area yourself.'

'He got the orchards as a dowry?'

'Exactly. Moretti bought them for him and got the loony sister off his hands for good.'

'Where was she before?'

'With the nuns. But they refused to keep her because, although she was docile enough—they taught her a bit of housekeeping and she helped in the kitchen—every so often she'd get out at night. Needless to say in the end she got pregnant, and after that they wanted her out. Moretti either had to take her home or have her locked up unless he could find some other way of fixing her up. Well, it seems he found it.'

'Then it is true . . .'

'As I say, he'd hardly have made it up, rogue though he is.'

'No, I mean . . . she told me she'd a child and for one reason and another I didn't believe her.'

'It's true enough, though I gather it didn't live long— just as well maybe. Well, there it is—not much use to us, I don't suppose. Berti was trying to make a bit of a saint out of Moretti on the grounds that he could have her put away in an asylum easily enough rather than putting out all that cash—is something the matter?'

'No, no . . . I was just wondering . . .'

'Of course it's true enough that the defence could make good use of a story like that if the worst comes to the worst, but what struck me more than anything is that there's a lot goes on in this town that I know nothing about.'

'And even that Berti knows nothing about.'

'I'm not so sure about that.'

'Hm. You said that according to him Moretti washed his hands of that poor woman once he'd got her married off?'

'So it seems.'

'Well, she told me she goes to see him regularly.'

'Probably made it up. Wishful thinking. How crazy do you think she is?'

'I don't know. As I said, she seems more childish than anything. I confess I more or less discounted everything she said but now I'm not so sure.'

'Well, if the old chap keeps her locked up—'

'He goes to play billiards.'

'You mean she gets out when he's—'

'Every week. It's not impossible. And when she told me she'd seen the girl go off down the road on Monday she said, "Maybe she went to see my brother."'

'She did? Well, it's beginning to sound plausible.'

'And you said it was her husband who found the body . . .'

The Marshal fell silent, staring into his coffee cup.

The dining-room was almost empty and there was a sound of crockery being washed in the kitchen. The television was still on with the sound turned low.

'Whichever way you look at it, it comes back to the same family,' said Niccolini after a moment, 'though what any of them could have had against that lass, I don't know—oh Lord, don't look now but here comes His Worship the Mayor-to-be . . .'

The Marshal had no need to look round since he could read the approach of Robiglio in Niccolini's narrowed eyes. Nevertheless it was a very different Robiglio from the version he had met the day before, and the Marshal was conscious of it as soon as they had shaken hands.

'Unfortunate business,' Robiglio said to Niccolini. 'I imagine this is what brought your colleague here, though you didn't care to mention it yesterday.'

'We didn't know—' began Niccolini, but Robiglio interrupted him with an arrogance he had been at some pains to conceal at their last meeting.

'Quite within your rights, of course, none of my business.' And he turned to call out: 'Tozzi! I shan't want a table tomorrow. I shall be leaving in the morning.' He gave them only a brief nod by way of salute and left them.

'Afternoon!' said Niccolini politely. 'And good riddance to you.' He added the last bit when Robiglio was out of earshot. 'Well, there goes another one who's not wanting to chat to me all of a sudden, not that it's any great loss in his case. I don't suppose he could tell us anything.'

'He seemed anxious enough to tell us one thing . . .' The Marshal's big eyes were still fixed on the door where Robiglio had gone out. 'He seemed to me to be letting us know he was leaving. I wonder why that should be.'

'You think so? Well, there's no reason why we should try and stop him.'

'None that we know of. I'd say that yesterday that was a worried man. He didn't like my being here. Now he knows why . . . I wonder where he's going.'

'I'll soon find out.' Niccolini jumped to his feet. 'I'll go and settle up and get Tozzi to tell me.'

'Let me . . .'

'You stay where you are. I'd better do a bit of public relations work. I shouldn't have been so sharp with him, you're right.'

'Even so, you must be my guest today.'

'I'll be your guest when I come to Florence.'

'But when—'

'In the year two thousand.' And he was gone.

The Marshal struggled into his overcoat, feeling as usual, rather heavy after his lunch, especially in comparison with Niccolini who always seemed to be bursting with pent-up energy. He came bounding back now, rubbing his hands together.

'That's done! And I can tell you where our friend's going. Switzerland!'

'Signorina Stauffer?' The door had opened only a crack and he could barely see who was behind it. 'Marshal Guarnaccia. May I come in?'

The door opened slowly. She kept her head down, but despite that and her glasses he could see that she had already been crying and he didn't look forward to telling her what he had to tell her. She led the way into a small sitting-room without speaking. The furniture was mostly worm-eaten antique and obviously came with the rented flat, but there were plenty of signs of the female occupants: some potted plants on a small table by the window, a row of postcards along the mantelpiece, a neatly folded pink sweater on the back of the chair. A young man was sitting on a battered velvet sofa in the centre of the room and there was a haze of cigarette smoke in the air. The Marshal had the feeling that he'd interrupted an intimate talk, no doubt on the subject of the missing friend. The young man got to his feet.

'Is it about Monica?'

The Marshal looked from him to the girl, waiting to learn who he was.

'My name's Corsari,' offered the young man, since the girl still didn't speak but stood nervously pulling at her fingers. 'I teach at the school . . .'

'I see.' And since nobody moved or offered him a seat it was the Marshal himself who suggested, 'Shall we sit down?' He took the chair where the sweater lay, balanced his hat on his knees and tried to avoid the anxious gazes fixed on him. 'I'm afraid it's bad news.'

Without looking at them directly, he was aware that the girl stiffened and drew in a sharp breath and that the young man moved closer to her on the sofa and put an arm round her shoulder.

'I knew something had happened to her, I knew . . .'

'Try to keep calm, Signorina.' The Marshal was more than a little grateful for the presence of the young man. 'Your friend's dead, I'm very sorry to tell you, and we need your help—'

'I warned her! I warned her to be careful!'

'To be careful of what? You thought she was in danger out there?'

'What am I going to do? What am I going to do?'

She sat rigidly upright on the sofa, trembling violently as if she would soon explode, but no explosion came. She suddenly crumpled and let out a low howl that sounded more animal than human.

'What am I going to do? Help me . . .' She fell back against the sofa with her eyes closed and heaved in a deep noisy breath that became a dry sob and was followed by others coming faster and faster.

The Marshal got to his feet. 'Stay close to her. I'll get her a glass of water—where's the kitchen?'

'Through there . . .'

He brought the water and handed the glass to the young man who was trying to hold her still. But her body was still heaving and her eyes, magnified by the heavy glasses, stared up at the Marshal as if she were still saying 'Help me'.

'I think she should lie down,' was all the help he could offer. 'Cover her up well, she should keep warm . . .'

The young man managed to get her to her feet, but he almost had to carry her as her legs were trembling too much to support her.

'Try talking to her for a while,' murmured the Marshal as they went through the door. 'It will be better for her if she can cry properly . . .'

Then he went and stood by the plants at the window, staring across at the house opposite which in this narrow street was only a few yards away. A woman was hanging washing on a wire strung on a pulley against the crumbling wall. After pegging out each piece she pulled on the wire which squeaked loudly. There were no other noises in the street and he could hear the murmur of the young man's voice punctuated by the girl's sobs. What had Robiglio called it? 'An unfortunate business.' Well, it was that all right. Two women passed below him walking in the narrow road since the pavements were blocked by parked cars. They were gossiping intently and a youngster on a moped coming in the opposite direction almost ran into them. One of the women turned to call after him: 'Look where you're going, thoughtless young idiot!' The boy made a rude gesture and carried on, wavering a little.

The noise from the bedroom had changed. The girl was speaking now, disjointedly but through what sounded like real tears which was a good thing. The Marshal wandered away from the window and stood observing the postcards on the mantelpiece. Most of them looked as if they came from Switzerland. What would Robiglio have gone to Switzerland for? According to what Tozzi had said, he went fairly often and Niccolini had immediately jumped to the conclusion that there was some connection there with the dead girl. Even so, it didn't do to lose sight of the obvious . . .

The young man reappeared.

'She's quieter now.'

'She might need a sedative tonight, nevertheless. Does she have a doctor here?'

'I'm not sure but I doubt it. I could call mine.'

'You've known them a long time, these girls?'

'Ever since they came here, more or less, since I teach at the school.'

'Then perhaps you could help me. I doubt if the Signorina can until she's calmer.' They could still hear her sobs which were muffled, probably by the bedclothes.

'If you think I can tell you anything useful—but perhaps you wouldn't mind telling me exactly what's happened to Monica . . .'

'She was strangled. To be more technically correct I should say throttled. There may well have been an attempt at rape beforehand but we won't know for sure until after the autopsy.'

'Do you mind if we sit down?' Young Corsari's face was white and he seemed dazed though he kept himself well under control. 'Where . . .?'

'Where did it happen? She was found near a terracotta factory where she was thought to have gone to work on Monday.'

'A factory . . .? But she worked for an artisan.'

'Yes, but it seems that every so often she went to this factory to keep her hand in at throwing.'

'I didn't know . . .'

'It had little enough importance until now. As you know her quite well perhaps you could tell me what Signorina Stauffer meant by saying "I warned her"?'

'It's difficult to explain.'

'Take your time.'

Corsari studied his hands for a moment and then the Marshal's face, as if trying to gauge his capacity for understanding. The Marshal's face told him nothing.

'I suppose it's a question of personality really . . .'

'Whose?'

'Monica's, of course. Elisabeth—well, you've seen her for yourself.'

'She's not very forthcoming.'

'You have to know her. People tend to think she's sullen or unfriendly but that's not the case. She's desperately shy, but once you've got her to trust you—anyway, it's Monica you want to know about. She's just the opposite, completely open and friendly. She's so lively and affectionate—I should be talking about her in the past tense, shouldn't I? But it's difficult . . . I expect her to burst in at the door any minute. She had a way of filling the house with life . . .' He looked around the room. 'It's so silent without her it seems like half a dozen people were missing instead of one. Do you understand what I mean?'

'I understand.'

'Then you can imagine that she attracted people.'

'Especially men?'

'I'm trying to come to that in a way that won't create any misunderstanding . . .'

'Go on.'

'I can't even say for sure whether I understood her completely myself, even though I've known her so long and have been in a position—she was friendly and affectionate with everyone, you see, and what Elisabeth felt was that she shouldn't be. There's a question of different cultures, too, of course. I've travelled a lot in northern Europe myself, so I know that it's possible, normal, for there to be affectionate friendships between men and women where no other sort of rapport ever enters into things. Here it's rather different. If a girl offers affectionate friendship to a man he's likely to take it for quite another sort of offer. Elisabeth felt, and I agree with her, that Monica should have adapted her behaviour to the country she was living in.'

'That seems reasonable.'

'Monica wouldn't accept it. She said her personality was what it was, that she enjoyed herself, and had no intention of being repressed. They quarrelled about it often, sometimes violently.'

'You don't think Signorina Stauffer might have simply been a little bit jealous, given that she doesn't have much of a gift for making friends herself?'

'Of course she was jealous. She was bound to be.'

A question of personality. A question of cultural differences. When was this young man going to come to the point? The Marshal observed him. He was perhaps twenty-five or twenty-six years old and good-looking. He seemed intelligent and cultured. The Marshal decided to bring him to the point, having already understood what it was.

'Were you a victim yourself of this sort of misunderstanding caused by the young lady's personality and these cultural differences?'

Corsari flushed. 'Yes, I suppose I was, though I think victim's too strong a word for it.'

'As you like. In any case you remained friends?'

'Certainly. There was no reason why I should give them up as friends because of that.'

'And then you got to know Signorina Stauffer better and transferred your affections to her, is that it?'

'I'm very fond of Elisabeth,' he said simply. 'But even so,

you mustn't think I had anything against Monica for the way things went. I said before I wasn't sure whether I completely understood her and it's true. Even afterwards, when I wasn't what you call the victim, I watched the same thing happen to other men without ever knowing for sure whether she did it in all innocence or whether there was a touch of . . . what shall I say . . .?'

'Malice?'

'That's too strong . . .'

Most plain speaking seemed to be too strong for him. The Marshal was revising his first good opinion of this man on the grounds that though he was very charming he really didn't seem to be much of a man at all. There was nothing in him you could get to grips with.

'Maybe she didn't know herself,' was his only comment.

Corsari's charming eyes lit up. 'Do you know, I think you're right. In any case, you couldn't call it malice. The most you could say is that she enjoyed teasing a little.'

'Somebody didn't take kindly to being teased a little, then.'

'You think that's . . .'

'What else do you expect me to think? Somebody killed her!'

'But nobody would go so far because of that, nobody normal!'

'So somebody happened along who wasn't normal. You said yourself she behaved that way with everybody. Things may have been precipitated by something further, like jealousy of another man—I presume that out of all these men she liked to tease a little there were one or two who succeeded with her?'

'No, no, it never went that far. At the most she would invite someone here for dinner and it would soon become clear that there was nothing further on offer, so they either disappeared or changed their expectations.'

'As you did?'

'Yes. I'm afraid that in spite of my efforts at explaining

you've got the wrong picture. It was all very light. Monica was a lovely girl and highly intelligent.'

'Would you mind giving me your name and address?'

'Certainly. I'll write it down for you.'

He got up and went to a small desk in the corner where there were writing materials in a drawer. It was evident that he was at home here. The Marshal stood up and waited. No further sound came from the bedroom and he wondered if the girl had exhausted herself with crying and fallen asleep.

'Here you are. I've given you my phone number at school as well, since I'm there most of the day.'

'You could also give me Monica Heer's home address and phone number if you know where to find them . . .'

'Of course. You'll have to inform her parents . . .'

'Yes.'

'It should be here somewhere.' He opened one or two more drawers, found what he was looking for and copied a second address on to the same piece of paper.

'Thank you. I'll be on my way.'

They passed the bedroom door which was ajar. The Marshal could see only a corner of the bed but a rustle and a faint sniff suggested that the girl was not asleep. The room was full of cigarette smoke.

'Remember what I said about a tranquillizer—and I don't think she should be left alone for some time.'

'I'll call my doctor now, and I can always sleep here on the sofa, I've done it before.'

The Marshal stared at him with bulging eyes but made no comment. Once the door had closed he stumped down the stairs since there was no lift, muttering to himself as he opened the street door: 'Well, I'm not convinced . . .'

But if anybody had asked him what it was he wasn't convinced about he would have had a hard time answering.

CHAPTER 5

The Marshal was descending the great staircase with difficulty. There was such a crush that he had already lost sight of his wife and the crowd was pressing him against the broad marble banister which was loaded for all its length with branches of bay and heaps of citrus fruit. The air was filled with the scent of lemons and the music of an opera by Verdi, though the Marshal couldn't remember which one. The staircase seemed to go on for ever and he had no hope of finding his wife until he reached the bottom of it. He was too hot in his uniform, and to make matters worse there was a rather elderly woman beside him with a brown velvet hat and protruding lips who was suffocating him with her perfume and kept prodding him in the ribs with her elbow as she gesticulated and shrilled her dissatisfaction with the way things had been organized.

'My dear, if they would just be more selective!'

The selection would presumably include herself but not overweight NCOs, to judge by the vicious little glance she gave the Marshal's uniform.

When at last he reached the bottom he spotted Dr Biondini shaking hands with people on the left, but the Marshal who was too far to the right had no hope of reaching him and didn't intend to try. All he wanted to do was to extricate himself somehow from the crowd that was carrying him along and turn round to see if his wife had got down. When he managed it he was surprised to find that she was tapping him on the shoulder, having reached the bottom before him.

'Did you speak to Dr Biondini?'

'How could I?' he grumbled. 'It's impossible. Where are we supposed to go now?'

'To the Sala Bianca. I asked someone. You really should have made the effort, Salva. He'll think it so rude . . .'

The Marshal only grunted and tried to fish for a handkerchief to mop his brow.

'We should have got here earlier,' whispered his wife.

'I don't see how if I was working . . .'

When they reached the Sala Bianca they were unable to get in and had to stand outside the room, hemmed in by the crowd, while an interminable speech was made by the politician who had been invited to open the exhibition and who was making the most of the opportunity to speak about anything other than the paintings, mostly, as far as the Marshal could make out, about himself and his early life in Florence. As if the exhibition hadn't provided enough of a security problem without this . . .

The Marshal glanced about him. He might be no expert but a crowd this size was a security risk, no matter how many men with metal detectors you had on the doors . . .

The thought was driven from his mind by a sharp poke in the back and a familiar voice.

'I can't hear a thing, let alone see. There really should be some provision for people who can't stand for any length of time. Can you get a glimpse? They say he's aged—I was a great friend of his mother's before *the* quarrel . . . you know what I mean . . . It *was* quite shocking, of course, and since the Princess considered herself to have been insulted in that woman's drawing-room I had no choice . . .'

'Let's get out of here,' muttered the Marshal.

'Salva! Shh . . .'

'Who, me? But if everybody else—'

'Shh!'

That was the woman behind. It was true that there was no hope of escape in reality since they were blocked in on all sides. There was nothing for it but to stick it out. It had been too long a day, that was the trouble. It was only four hours or so since he had left Niccolini to come back and visit Signorina Stauffer, but it seemed more like four days. And at this rate they'd be lucky to get home to their supper before eight-thirty or nine . . .

'. . . *the questions and problems inherent in the cultural, environ-mental and artistic heritage of the city known—not without reason —in the last century, as the Athens of Italy. In the words of Carducci . . .*'

Just as well he'd managed to phone the Captain before coming over here, though he hadn't been able to tell him much apart from the girl's home address. After all, there was knothing concrete to tell, nothing cut and dried that you could put in a report or even explain on the phone. Not that the Captain expected anything unreasonable.

'I'm just interested in your impressions at this point . . .'

Which was all very well, but the Marshal wasn't a great one for explaining things. You needed someone with brains for that sort of thing. Someone with the gift of the gab like this fellow sounding off now . . .

'. . . *Florence at the end of the thirteenth century could in a way be said to have anticipated what, at the end of the seventeen hundreds, five centuries later, was the atmosphere of revolutionary France. The Guilds became republics within the Republic, and the artisans, while having no active part in the government . . .*'

'If you have any ideas, even in a general way . . .'

But the Marshal never had ideas. His mind was full of images that jostled each other without resolving themselves into anything definite: the hostile gaze of a red-stained man, his feet buried in clay shavings; the silent, smelly little room where Tina's cat warmed itself against a terracotta bowl of ashes; the dreariness of a high black wall in the rain . . . What was the point of trying to explain stuff like that, even if he'd been capable of it? It may well have been to cover his embarrassment that he had said, rather prematurely, he thought on reflection, 'We might need the Fiscal Police . . .'

'Really? You mean—'

'I don't know, it's nothing definite—I've no proof that there's anything . . . we'd better wait and see.'

Thank goodness the Captain hadn't insisted but had asked him instead how things were going with Niccolini. That at least was something he could answer.

'All right, I think. We're getting along. At any rate I get along fine with him and I hope he doesn't mind having me around . . . It was a bit difficult at first . . .'

'I'm convinced you'll work well together. Now if you'll give me the girl's home address I'll see about getting in touch with her parents.'

He wouldn't have been so convinced, thought the Marshal, if he'd seen them that morning. Still, he was right, after all. The Captain was an intelligent man.

And so, if it came to that, was that young fellow . . . what was his name? Corsari. Hm. Very smooth hands he'd had, and something else . . . his ears, that was it. Funny . . . he couldn't remember having noticed them at the time but now he could see them as clearly as if they'd been in front of him. Clean and pale and so sharply modelled they might have just come out of a mould. What was it Niccolini had said? You're the sort of person who notices things . . . a fat lot of good that was, noticing things that were irrelevant. Those great moulds of Sestini's up in that damp, freezing room with the rain coming in at a broken window . . . he hadn't caught on to what they were, though of course they were in pieces. Must have been drying there above the kiln. Funny how you could see those great big red pots in gardens all over Tuscany and never wonder how on earth they were made . . . That was what the half-empty room smelled of . . . damp plaster, and the rest of the rooms had the clean earthy smell of wet clay. All of it so cold and then the sudden heat of the kiln when they fired . . . That couldn't be very often. Most of the time it must be a pretty uncomfortable place to work, especially in winter, but they were used to it. Not the girl, though. It couldn't have been much fun working in that desolate, ramshackle factory in winter, especially when it was empty. Hadn't he thought that same thing already? No . . . that was to do with Berti's place when he'd thought she surely couldn't have stood out there in the rain waiting—well, she'd found a way round that because there was Tina. Had she found a way round it at Moretti's too?

There she didn't even have Berti to drive her into the town to get a hot meal. Berti could have picked her up there, of course, if he'd wanted to . . . but no, Niccolini said she hadn't turned up to eat. Funny that she'd never missed before so that nobody realized she sometimes went to Moretti's. It would have been logical, after all, for Berti to have given her a lift. What other solution could she have found that one day . . . There was Robiglio's house across the way . . . He remembered there being a face looking out there too and tried to imagine the pale indistinct figure he had seen, beckoning . . . too far-fetched altogether. Must be something simpler, something more obvious. What if she was killed before lunch? That could be it, in which case Berti perhaps did go there and so knew . . . Well, the autopsy would tell. Even so, he felt he was missing something, something that had already crossed his mind right at first, just as it had crossed his mind that if Berti kept his place locked up and wouldn't give her a key . . . No. It was there somewhere but he couldn't grasp it. No doubt it would come back to him when he wasn't trying to remember. At least he could stop at Berti's tomorrow and ask him outright whether he usually picked the girl up and drove her to the restaurant when she was working at Moretti's. He might be a shifty character but the Marshal had a feeling that he wouldn't risk telling a downright lie if he was asked the right question. Had she given him the treatment, the teasing job? Probably she considered him too old to bother with. No doubt the young brigadier would have got the full works if it hadn't been that Niccolini had always been present— and there was an odd business! Niccolini had a head on his shoulders and you'd think he'd have cottoned on to her tricks. Of course, in a way he had, but like young Corsari, he had insisted that it was all very light and charming . . . 'Teases him a bit but nothing out of place.' But something was out of place all right. For one thing it couldn't be true that some man or other hadn't succeeded with her. At that age she must surely have a lover—unless she'd been crossed and was going through a bad patch, taking her revenge. But no, the bitterness would have shown through—and young Corsari would have known by this time, having remained friends with the girls for so long. And since he was so anxious to defend her behaviour he'd have been the first to offer thàt as an excuse. He was no fool.

'Well, there's something wrong somewhere . . . must be me that's a fool if I can't see it!'

'*Salva!*'

'What?'

He came to himself with a start and found himself being gazed at reproachfully by a boneless-looking saint with her mouth hanging slightly open. He blinked and looked around him as if the brilliant chandeliers high above him had just been switched on.

'Salva . . .' murmured his wife, blushing in her embarrassment. 'Whatever's the matter with you? You've been scowling at everybody for the last twenty minutes and now you're talking to yourself. . .'

'I am? Well, what of it? Nobody can have noticed in all this chaos.'

'Lots of people noticed. And you haven't so much as glanced at a single painting.'

If that whey-faced saint with her mouth open was anything to go by the Marshal reckoned he hadn't missed much, but he didn't say so. He made a valiant effort at craning his neck and standing on tiptoe and managed to glimpse a few gilded frames over and around the crowd of people. He hadn't even noticed, to tell the truth, that at some point the long-winded speech had come to an end and he had been carried along with the rest to view the exhibition.

One good thing was that they had lost the velvet-hatted woman somewhere along the way. After a moment he found that the crowd had pushed them aside and rolled on so that for the first time he had a whole painting before him and no heads in between. He stood still, staring at a curious little figure to the right of it and then let his gaze roll over the rest. If he stopped off at Berti's on the way tomorrow, might it not be wise to have another word with Tina while he was at it? Crazy though she had seemed, much of the things as she had told him that he had been able to check on had turned out to be true. There was no knowing what else—

'Ah, Marshal! Signora, good evening. Well, Marshal, I see you're admiring the Parmigianino. Lovely, isn't it? A very original work and so modern, of course, for its time.'

They both shook hands with Dr Biondini and the Marshal's big eyes widened in perplexity.

'You were quite engrossed in it,' said Biondini, smiling. 'Now I feel guilty for having interrupted you.'

'Ah . . .' And he turned to the picture again, this time seeing it whole and wondering what he should say. 'Well . . . but isn't it . . . the neck looks a bit on the long side to my way of thinking . . .' He felt his wife's fingers digging into his arm and thought he'd probably said something he shouldn't.

'Of course!' Biondini laughed. 'You're quite right. In fact it's known as the Madonna with the long neck.'

His wife's fingers relaxed their grip.

'I'm afraid it's a terrible squeeze here this evening, but there are some lovely things to eat and drink if you can only get to them—and if you can drag yourself away from the Madonna with the long neck! You certainly do notice things, but then I suppose it's your job, isn't it? You are quite a character!'

'Oh, Salva, you really are a one, and no mistake!'

'Who, me?'

It was almost ten o'clock but what with eating so late after the opening his wife had only just finished clearing away and sat down beside him on the settee where he was watching television, or pretending to watch it. The film had already started when he'd come in from the kitchen and turned it on and he hadn't the faintest idea what it was about.

'I give up!'

He became aware that his wife was knitting with some agitation, stopping every so often to count stitches ferociously. Something was up.

'What's the matter?'

'Never mind, if you're too tired to talk about it.'

'Talk about what?'

'About what? But if I've tried to tell you once I've tried five times—about the boys having to go right across the city with practically nothing in their stomachs to a gymnasium that's half the size of this room just to run about in the dust. They'd be better off staying at home!'

'Run about in the dust . . .?'

'What else can they do in a room that size? And they call that physical education! If it weren't so far away they could at least have their lunch but with only an hour between that and the last lesson they've no time for more than a sandwich, the buses being what they are. Anyway, I think you should come with me to the meeting.'

'What meeting?'

'Oh, Salva! The meeting I'm telling you about if you'll only come back to earth for a minute. It looks better if you come. You haven't once set foot in the school. People will think they haven't got a father.'

'But everybody round here knows me . . .'

'That's not the point. You should show an interest. It's at six-thirty tomorrow night.'

'At six-thirty? I won't be here . . . at least I don't think so.'

'You're not going to be out all day again?'

'Mmm.' She gave out a dramatic sigh and counted some more stitches but that seemed to be the end of the matter. They watched the film in silence for a quarter of an hour before she spoke again.

'Who's that? That's not his wife . . .'

'Eh? Whose wife?'

'*His* wife. The one we just saw leaving on a plane. The woman we got a glimpse of at the airport was blonde. Wasn't his wife a brunette and taller?'

'I've no idea.'

Another dramatic sigh.

'Your mother was right, God rest her soul. Half the time you're asleep on your feet.'

'Mmm.'

They went to bed straight after the news. Before going into their bedroom his wife went in as usual to cover up the youngest boy who always slept sprawled out with the blankets trailing down to the floor. The older boy slept huddled in a heap with his head almost invisible. The Marshal hovered at the door, the expression in his eyes like that of a jealous mother cat, though he didn't go in. Despite his wife's remark about his not taking enough interest, the two plump dark-haired boys were the centre of his existence. It was true that his wife was the one who did everything including giving them a hiding when they'd been up to mischief, but then she would always add, 'If I tell Papa what you've done, you'll get a *real* hiding!' And they would beg her not to. Naturally, she would tell him on the quiet and he would play up to his menacing image by glaring at them with huge threatening eyes, but the real hiding never happened. He was incapable of laying a finger on them.

When they were settled in bed and his wife had turned out the lamp he suddenly said in the darkness, 'Maybe it's because I eat too much.'

'What is?'

'You said I seem to be asleep on my feet. Maybe I eat too much and that's what makes me dozy.'

'Don't be ridiculous.'

'All right.'

'It's because you've got something on your mind. Is it work?'

'Perhaps.'

She didn't insist. He had never got into the habit of talking about work problems with her, in part because he tried not to think about them when the working day was over, which wasn't easy given that they lived in the barracks. But it was also because they had been separated for so long when he had been sent to Florence and she had had to stay with the boys down in Syracuse because there was his sick mother to look after. He had got into the habit of brooding on things by himself. Even so, after a moment he sighed and said, 'You're right. I've got an unpleasant business on my hands . . .'

'Is that why you've been out so much?'

'Yes.'

'Try not to think about it. Get a good night's sleep.'

Easier said than done. When he did drop off his head was still filled with those same images of the rainy pottery town, and nobody could have been more surprised than he was when he awoke feeling refreshed and light as if the whole business had been resolved in the simplest possible terms during the night. If he had dreamed he had no recollection of it and he found it very difficult to come back to the reality of having understood nothing at all and of being back at square one where he had been the day before. Even when he had reminded himself of the fact, the light, confident feeling remained.

'Well, you certainly look more cheerful this morning,' his wife remarked as he sat down before his big cup of milky coffee and a brioche. 'Did you sleep well?'

'I must have done . . .' There was no explaining it, and what was more he had the feeling that what was at the bottom of it was that he must have remembered during the night the fact that had eluded him yesterday. Again he was convinced that it was linked to the girl's being locked out in the rain, but if he had indeed remembered during the night he recalled nothing of it now.

Before leaving, he went into his office to fill in the daily sheet which he hadn't managed to get to the evening before because of the exhibition.

'Are you going to be out all day again?' Brigadier Lorenzini, though perfectly capable of managing everything in his absence, looked as if he and the lads were being left orphans.

'I'll get back as early as I can this afternoon.'

But he wasn't to see his office again for a long time, if only he'd known it. He got into his greatcoat and, after a glance out of the window at the bright wintry weather, fished about in the pockets for his sunglasses and put them on. At the bottom of the stairs he greeted the park-keepers in their office on the ground floor, and came out blinking even behind his dark glasses into the bright day. His battered little car was parked in deep shadow alongside the squad car and the van on the gravel just outside the door. As he got in and started the engine he glanced over the laurel bushes at the glittering marble bell-tower and the red-domed cathedral wreathed in a pale bluish mist and remembered that yesterday should have been his day off. It would have been nice to be free today to take a turn around the peaceful tree-lined paths in the Boboli Gardens here, pausing to look at the goldfish swimming around below the fountain in the green lake, or to sit for a while on a warm stone bench in one of the sunny arbours guarded by white statues of Roman soldiers. He would even have enjoyed a walk in the centre with his wife to look at the elegant shops they would never be able to afford to go into.

'Well,' he muttered to himself, 'have to wait till you're on your pension. Let's hope at least that the weather stays like this even out there . . .'

If anything, there seemed to be rather more ground mist about once he was on the open road and following the railway line, and he wound up the window which he had left open until then. It seemed a few degrees cooler, though that might have been his imagination. However, the sky remained empty and bright. When he pulled over and parked outside Berti's place the cottage with the pile of junk and plastic bags beside it looked even more dilapidated and dirty in the sunlight than it had in the grey November rain that had softened and camouflaged it.

There was no other car there and the metal shutter was rolled down covering the door and window of the studio. Before he had even switched off his engine Tina's pale round face appeared behind the small barred window, smiling vacantly, as though she had been expecting him. When he got out and tapped at the door he could hear her shuffling footsteps already approaching and she opened the door to him readily, one eye smiling at him with childish pleasure, the other drifting.

'Good morning,' began the Marshal, 'I won't come in—'

But she was shuffling away from him, pretending not to hear, and he had no choice but to take off his dark glasses and follow her, holding his breath against the stench in the narrow corridor.

'You can sit on the chair where you sat before.'

He could imagine her saying the same thing to the Swiss girl, pathetic in her pleasure at receiving somebody. The house was exactly as it had been, everything severely tidy but nothing looking fresh and clean, though that might have been a psychological effect of the smell.

'I wanted to ask you about your brother—your brother is Moretti, is that right?'

'That's right.' Her eyes lit up at the mention of him.

'Why don't you sit down, too?'

She pulled another hard chair away from the table and sat down facing him with her hands in her lap like an obedient child.

'When you go to see him, do you go to his house.'

She shook her head. 'He hasn't got a house.'

'I see.' Did he tell her that to keep her off his back? At any rate this wasn't the moment to disillusion her since he seemed to be the only light in her life. 'You go to the factory, then?'

'That's right. But only when there's nobody else there, so nobody knows. You won't tell *him*?'

'No, no . . .' He thought for a moment. 'He doesn't come to see you here.'

'For a while he did but I don't think he'll come any more, not now.'

'Why is that?'

'He liked to look at the Signorina but now she won't be coming any more, will she?'

'No, she won't be coming any more.'

'Will they put her in the cemetery?'

'Yes.'

'That's where they put my baby. Will she be put near my baby?'

'No, a long way away, near her own house.'

'That is a long way, she told me. But not across the sea.'

'No, not across the sea. Did your brother come last week to see the Signorina?'

'Yes. He used to say how pretty she was. He used to say that she liked him and sometimes she used to go and see him. She used to smile at him, and at me, too. She used to smile at everybody.'

'That's right,' the Marshal said, 'she did.'

'Even Robiglio, and he's a spy.'

'Robiglio? He came here, too?'

'No.'

'Then how do you know?'

'My brother told me.'

'Well, perhaps she didn't know he was a spy. Do you know what a spy is?'

'Somebody wicked. He was sick afterwards, my grandma told me. She used to say he was as sick as a dog afterwards and that he tried to hide his face from her and that the whole room was full of blood and they drank all the wine in the house.'

'Who did?'

'*They* did.'

'You don't know who they were? Do you know why the room was full of blood?'

'No.'

'You weren't here?'

'Yes, I was.'

'But you can't remember what happened?'

'I was asleep.'

The Marshal would have been tempted to dismiss all this as the ramblings of a lost mind, but he had a double reason for not doing so. First of all, he had thought the same thing about her story of the baby which had turned out to be true, and secondly because he remembered that Robiglio had been involved in something nasty during the war. If this was the something concerned, then there must be a more reliable source of information somewhere and there was no point in pursuing it with Tina. Perhaps it was this vague and disturbing story that caused the feeling of anxiety he had felt yesterday to return and obliterate his morning optimism. A feeling that if they didn't get there in time something was going to happen. He got to his feet.

'Are you going away?' Tina looked about her as if hoping to find something to distract and delay him as the picture of her baby had done, but he put on his hat and moved to the door.

She shuffled after him pulling at his coat sleeve.

'Aren't you going to touch me?'

'What?'

'Aren't you going to do something to me?'

'No . . .'

He heard her draw in a sharp breath and her shuffling steps came to a sudden halt. He was already in the corridor and he turned to look down at her, surprised that his answer should have caused such a strong reaction. But he was mistaken. Her habituated ear had caught a sound he hadn't noticed and her face was red with fright.

The front door was opening and silhouetted against the bright light from outside the Marshal saw a small dark figure holding something bulky. When the door closed and they were all enclosed in the evil-smelling gloom he saw that this must be Tina's husband standing as still as a suspicious animal and staring at them in silence, a dark, rat-like little man in a greasy black beret, carrying a big bundle of grass under one arm.

'Good morning.'

The Marshal's greeting was left hanging in the air and nobody moved. Then the small man's mouth widened in a threatening leer directed at Tina and showing two widely spaced brown teeth. Without a word, he turned and opened the door of the room where the animals were kept and vanished.

The Marshal went to the front door and opened it, turning to take his leave of Tina, but she, too, had disappeared. He went out, blinking into the daylight and put on his sunglasses.

There was still no sign of Berti and he hovered there a moment outside the studio, watching the traffic stream by and wondering whether to wait.

A muffled, high-pitched sound behind him made him turn and look back at Tina's house, frowning. He saw nothing but the little black cat, or rather its eyes, glittering in the gloom behind the bars. Perhaps he had imagined the noise. He strained his ears but there was nothing but the dull sound of the traffic. This place was getting on his nerves. The anxiety was rising inside him no matter how he tried to reason it away. But the noise came again and this time there was no possibility of his having imagined it. A frightened wail, desolate and barely human. His first thought was that the hare he had seen fattening in the barrel was being slaughtered, but he knew it wasn't true even before he remembered the big bundle of grass. Then he heard a man's voice raised in anger though the words were indistinct. He caught only the odd phrases:

'How often have I told you? Well? Well? Imbecile! Keep your stupid mouth shut!'

Then the terrified wail again.

He took a few steps towards the door and then stopped. If he went in there and intervened—even supposing somebody opened up for him, which was unlikely—he would only make matters worse. He couldn't stay there for ever and once he left . . . What was the use?

He got into the car. He couldn't stand to wait here for Berti, Niccolini would have to see to it.

But as he drove round the big curve the first thing he saw was Berti, coming down the steps of Moretti's factory with his slow spidery walk and a stack of plates in his arms. Parked below the wall in front of the terrace was a truck, and the big man in the woollen hat was lowering a huge red pot down to someone standing in it surrounded by heaps of straw. The Marshal braked, putting on his indicator. The only way to get over there was to turn in in front of Robiglio's gates as Berti had done. He glanced down the drive at the big house with the seven lavatories but no one was looking out today, as far as he could see. He turned and drove across to Moretti's, parking in front of the truck. The blue car was parked behind it and Berti was loading plates into the boot, but the Marshal didn't approach him at once. Having got out of his car on the side near the wall, he was able to see something which had been invisible from the road because the truck had been in the way. Someone had used a can of red spray paint, probably during the night, to write in huge uneven letters along the wall below the terrace the word MURDERER.

The Marshal was standing at the window in Niccolini's office looking down at the square. The rainwashed bronze statue of the partisan shone in the winter sunlight, but for the rest the town had the air of someone facing the day unwashed and uncombed after getting reluctantly out of bed. The sunshine only served to accentuate the crumbling façades and peeling shutters whose brown paint had faded almost to grey under the frequent rains. In Niccolini's office, at least, everything was spick and span. The walls were newly whitened, the desk polished, and a tall rubber plant of military bearing stood sentry in one corner of the floor.

'That's done!' announced Niccolini, bursting into the room rubbing his hands together. 'And I think we've done right. I'm sure we have. Always best to be on the safe side.'

The Marshal's anxiety subsided a little. He had suggested to Niccolini that they put a guard on Moretti's factory, and Niccolini, when he heard about the accusation sprayed on the wall, had agreed that it might well be necessary, saying, 'I don't like the sound of that, I don't like the sound of it at all . . .'

By this time a squad car was on its way to the factory and the Marshal felt able to recount something of what he had discovered since the two of them had parted company the previous day. His recent chat with Berti outside the factory had produced nothing concrete. Berti had not denied that he had picked up the girl from Moretti's on previous occasions to drop her at the restaurant, since it was on his way home, but swore he hadn't gone there the day she died.

'Why didn't you, if you usually did?'

'I didn't feel like it. No reason in particular. She could look after herself for once, I thought.'

'Did you? Well, you were wrong.'

'Be reasonable, Marshal, be reasonable. I couldn't have known.'

Which was no doubt true, and there was little the Marshal could say.

'Do you reckon he was lying?' asked Niccolini, after listening without comment.

'Yes and no.' The Marshal hesitated. 'For some reason I believe him when he said he didn't go there that day. He didn't hesitate for a second in denying it, almost as if . . . as if he were on absolutely safe ground, but . . .'

'But?'

'With Berti I never get the feeling that he's telling me lies, more a feeling that he's not telling me anything. Somehow or other he manages to skate round the truth . . . After all, he did say in the first place that the girl probably went to Moretti's that day. What he didn't tell us was that he knew she'd gone there, that it had been agreed beforehand. And that makes me wonder if his not picking her up there had also been agreed beforehand.'

'Well, you could be right, but why?'

'So as not to be in somebody's way, maybe, somebody who had plans for her that day . . . It seems Moretti used to go round to Berti's place when she was there, ogling her.'

'I wouldn't have thought it of him. But in any case, Moretti was at the restaurant that day, not at the factory.'

'I know. Nobody was at the factory if we're to believe all we're told, but somebody killed the girl, even so.'

'Hm. You've seen to the business of informing the parents?'

'I've left it in the Captain's hands. I went to the flat . . .'

It wasn't easy now to explain that business of the girl's odd behaviour if only because it was seen through the eyes of that good-looking young man, Corsari, whom the Marshal hadn't liked at all—he couldn't explain why that was, either. He did his best but he didn't make much of a job of it, and he couldn't have been more amazed when at the end of his jumbled and hesitant account Niccolini sat back and slapped a hand down on the desk.

'Well I'll be damned! Trust you to get at the truth. I said you were one for noticing things and I was right! I wouldn't have thought I could be taken in in the same way twice, but it looks like I'm a bigger fool than I thought, and at my time in life, too, when I've had more women than hot dinners!'

That must be a lot, the Marshal thought, amazed at this new aspect of his energetic colleague. But what did Niccolini imagine he had noticed?

'I'm not sure I—'

But Niccolini rolled over him happily.

'The first time it happened to me was in Rome—I'm

talking about a good few years ago, and in those days this uniform—and even more so full dress uniform—drew the women like flies round a honey-pot. Don't get me wrong, I'm fond of my wife and my boys are everything to me, but I've never turned down a pretty woman yet, I love them all. Well, this one was an officer's wife and a risky proposition, but she was a beauty though a few years older than me, a real charmer. It began on a "bring me—fetch me— carry me" basis and I thought to myself, "All right, I'll go along with you, the moment will come." Well, the moment came all right, when she asked me to drive her home one day and invited me in for a drink. We even got as far as the bedroom before she sprang it on me. There I was all bright-eyed and bushy-tailed ready to uphold the honour of the army when she turns around and says, "I'm afraid you're wasting your time if that's what you have in mind. Not that I have anything against men as friends, but they do nothing for me in erotic terms. As far as that's concerned, I prefer women." You could have knocked me down with a feather. I laugh about it now, young fool that I was, but I can tell you I was livid, livid! She had to find somebody else to do her fetching and carrying after that!'

'But the husband . . .' ventured the Marshal, his solemn eyes almost popping out of his head.

'Preferred little boys. Marriage of convenience. And if that young man you told me about hangs around with two lesbians, then he's probably neither flesh nor fowl himself, whether he knows it or not.'

'So that's what they found out when they were invited to dinner . . .'

'And I can just see their faces.'

'Good God . . . I think, if you don't mind, I'd better give that young man a ring. I wouldn't like to be mistaken on something like this.'

'There's no mistake, you mark my words, but ring him by all means if you want to.'

The Marshal fished out the slip of paper from the notebook in his top pocket and tried the school number, since it was morning. Corsari wasn't there, having rung in to say he was taking the day off. He tried Signorina Stauffer's number and Corsari himself answered the phone.

'I thought I should stay with Elisabeth,' he explained, 'she's in rather a bad way.'

'Did you call a doctor?'

'Yes, and he gave her something so at least she got some sleep during the night. I'm wondering whether to suggest she go home once she's fit to travel, if that's all right with you.'

'I'd rather she didn't leave for the moment, especially as I need to take a written statement from her as soon as she's feeling well enough . . . I wanted to ask you about Signorina Stauffer's relationship with Monica Heer . . .'

'Yes? What about it?'

'I . . .' The Marshal glanced over at Niccolini, wishing that he'd asked him to deal with this. 'Were they . . . Was it an intimate relationship—I mean, were they . . .'

'Lesbians? Of course. I thought you'd realized that from the beginning.'

'I don't see why,' the Marshal defended himself.

'Perhaps not, although from our conversation I must say you gave me the impression—you even asked me if the quarrels caused by Monica's bringing men home were caused by jealousy, so . . .'

'I see. And that's what Signorina Stauffer meant by her warning. She considered her friend's behaviour risky?'

'Yes.'

'Thank you.'

The Marshal put the phone down and rubbed a hand over his face, embarrassed and very annoyed with himself.

Niccolini was busy searching through a file.

'You're not the only one who's been busy—here we are. I rang the Medico-Legal Institute first thing this morning —too early of course for anything more than the on-the-spot findings of yesterday, since it'll be a few days before they've done any analyses. At any rate, we know she died at lunch-time. The doctor reckons towards one o'clock but to cover himself he's saying officially between twelve and two. She ate something almost immediately before death, certainly bread, probably a sandwich of some sort, we'll have to wait for an analysis to know exactly—but that does tie in with Berti's having planned in advance not to take her to the restaurant. I doubt she'd have eaten a sandwich at that time otherwise. There's no question that she didn't die where we found her and that she wasn't wearing the jeans we found her in—or at least they certainly weren't fastened. She wasn't a virgin, so she must have given it a try at some point before going the other way—and that brings us to the rape business: there are scratches on the breasts and thighs which suggest that it was attempted but there's no trace of its having been successful. Nothing to analyse under the nails which were scrubbed clean, so if she put up a fight it wasn't much of one, didn't have a chance.'

'Funny . . .' murmured the Marshal. 'Usually—'

'Wait, there's a good reason. She took quite a severe blow on the back of the head before she died, so it's possible that she was knocked down and lost consciousness right at the start of the attack. What *is* funny is that after that, whoever attacked her didn't succeed in raping her but, maybe infuri-ated by her lack of response—this is only guesswork—not only strangled her but beat her head against something hard, probably the floor as there were no sharp corners involved, after she was dead. Now I don't know if that suggests to you what it suggests to me . . . What do you think?'

'That he didn't have rape in mind, that he was expecting cooperation and was baffled and enraged not to get it. I suppose that's what you mean and it ties in with her be-haviour. Even so . . .'

'Yes. Even so, I'd say he wasn't right in the head to have reacted that strongly. Like a wild beast. Of course, people like that sometimes have the appearance of being quite normal until something provokes them. I've known cases before. Anyway, that's the lot for the moment.'

Like a wild beast . . .

'I ought to tell you,' the Marshal said, 'that on my way here I also went to see Tina . . .'

CHAPTER 6

'I'll tell you what.' Niccolini was marching up and down behind his desk between the rubber plant and a filing cabinet in the opposite corner. 'We need more facts and less gossip, that's what we need. I'm not just referring to Tina, either. I was thinking the same thing yesterday but with Robiglio in mind—and if it turns out there's a connection there, then all the more reason . . .'

The Marshal's big eyes followed him back and forth, wishing he would sit down but realizing that he had already required him to be silent and listen, and that to ask him to be still as well was asking too much. So he said nothing.

'I want to know exactly what Moretti's deal with that peasant farmer was over his sister. I want to know what Sestini meant by saying you can't get away with it twice, and I want to know what our friend Robiglio was up to during the war because it just might stop him getting elected if it's raked up now, and who knows whether that young girl found out something—what do you think?'

'I think,' said the Marshal slowly, 'as I've already said . . . that there's something more recent . . . Still, I agree with you, we do need facts, only I'm afraid nobody's going to give us any.'

Niccolini stopped marching and smiled broadly.

'Now there you're wrong. I made my mind up on this yesterday, and when I make my mind up I get busy. There had to be somebody in this town who wasn't involved in any of its feuds and scandals and I've found him. It was my brigadier's mother who put me on to him. She's lived here all her life and though she's too young to remember much about the war she was able to tell me where to look. Dr Arnolfo Frasinelli's our man!' He sat down at last, rubbing his hands together with satisfaction. 'Eighty-six years old but they say he's as quick as a twenty-year-old, knows the history of everybody in this place, especially as for years he was a GP, and takes no nonsense from any of them. We're going along to meet him shortly, and with any luck he'll be able to explain at least some of this lot.'

With the flourish of a conjuror Niccolini whipped open his desk drawer and spread a bunch of papers under the Marshal's nose. 'You told me to expect them and here they are, for what they're worth.'

'Anonymous letters . . .'

'Exactly. And not one of them any help unless Frasinelli can enlighten us. Take a look through.' And he carried on marching up and down behind the Marshal's chair.

The first letter the Marshal took from the pile was written with a ballpoint pen in capitals on a sheet of lined paper torn from a child's exercise book. Only two lines were written at the top: ASK MORETTI WHERE HE GOT THE MONEY TO BUY LAND WHEN HE WAS IN DEBT. He turned the paper over but there was nothing else. The next one he picked up caused him to frown. It was not a letter at all but a sheet of tracing paper on which someone had used a thick paintbrush and brownish-black paint to draw a large swastika.

'Man of few words,' commented Niccolini, seeing the Marshal's puzzled frown.

'It's not that so much . . . I imagine it refers to Robiglio, but the tracing paper . . .'

'That's no mystery. Most of the potters who do majolica use it. They trace designs, then prick through all the lines of the drawing with a pin and dust charcoal through it on to a pot. I've seen it done many a time—and that's not paint but a metal oxide for painting over glaze.'

'Could be Berti, then . . .'

'Or a dozen other people.'

The Marshal went on reading and Niccolini got up and began striding about again.

ASK MORETTI WHAT GOES ON AT ROBIGLIO'S ON FRIDAY NIGHTS.

The Marshal looked up, inquiring.

'That one's no mystery.' Niccolini was looking over his shoulder. 'Gambling. Heard all about that from my predecessor when I arrived here. A select group of Robiglio's friends, industrialists from Prato and Florence, get together at his house each Friday night. Some pretty large sums change hands, they say Robiglio's the banker.'

'You've never done anything about it?'

'There's nothing I can do. Oh, my predecessor tried. Called on him one Friday night on some pretext or other and there they all were, large as life. Whisky and cigars, green baize cloth, the whole works. They were playing baccarat. But there was no sign of any money, not so much as a scrap of paper to indicate that any money changed hands there. Robiglio, cool as a fish on ice, offered the Marshal a drink and even invited him to join them as it was a friendly game, no money involved, just a group of pals passing a pleasant evening. There wasn't a thing he could do.'

'Hm.' The Marshal laid the letter aside and read on.

ERNESTO ROBIGLIO SPY SS HANGMAN MURDERER DON'T LET HIM GET AWAY TWICE.

And the next one:

IF YOU LOCK UP THE WHOLE FAMILY IN THE VILLA YOU'LL BE DOING THIS TOWN A FAVOUR.

This last one was signed '10 Respectable Citizens.'

'The ten respectable citizens forgot to tell us which family they were talking about,' remarked Niccolini, still looking over the Marshal's shoulder.

'What do they mean by the villa?'

'The asylum, of course.'

'Of course. Listen, Niccolini . . . you couldn't sit down a minute, could you?'

'That's what my wife always says! "Can't you just sit still for one minute?" She's right, of course. Here I am, sitting still for as long as it lasts. What's the problem?'

'The problem is that these letters are written by people who seem to think we know as much about the goings-on in this town as they do—those of them that aren't pure nastiness, that is—'

'You're right, you're right—nod's as good as a wink—'

'But you're doing it, too,' protested the Marshal, leaning forward a little with his big hands planted on his knees and staring hard at Niccolini with a vague hope of quietening him down. No doubt Niccolini's wife had been trying to do the same thing for years. 'Tell me about the asylum. All about it.'

'I showed you the place only yesterday!' roared Niccolini '—eh no, no, it was raining so you couldn't see it, you're right.'

But the Marshal remembered now.

'You mean the Medici villa up on the hill . . . When I first came here on the bus it was full of people who were going to an asylum. So that's the place.'

'That's the place, though who our respectable citizens want us to shut up in there I don't know.'

'Most of these letters, as far as I can see,' pointed out the Marshal, 'are directed against Robiglio and Moretti.'

'Yes, but why? If you ask me, everybody in this town knows by now who did for the girl, so by rights the letters should all be aimed at the same person.'

'Not necessarily.' The Marshal looked down at the letters spread on the desk. He didn't like anonymous letters but experience had taught him their logic, such as it was. 'There are plenty of people only too ready to make use of a situation like this to do the dirty on somebody they don't like.'

'Or on some political opponent who looks like winning the elections?'

'That, too. There might well be no truth in the accusations against Robiglio but even a short-lived scandal would probably put paid to his chances. Look at this one: NO MORE FASCIST MAYORS. ROBIGLIO IS A MURDERER. That's surely someone hoping we'll rake up Robiglio's past during our investigation rather than a reference to the murdered girl. The ones directed at Moretti are probably more to the point.'

'Except he's the one person who couldn't have been at the factory when it happened.'

'You've checked his alibi?'

'Double-checked it—Listen, we ought to be on our way to visit our oldest inhabitant. We'll take these letters with us and I'll tell you the rest of my news on the way.'

There was no doubt that Niccolini had been busy the day before. The Marshal was amazed as ever by his energy and slightly ashamed that he himself seemed to have achieved so little. Sitting in the passenger seat, gazing at the darkened landscape through his sunglasses, he listened in silence as Niccolini rattled on, emphasizing his remarks with one hand and steering with the other.

'So I telephoned these clients of Moretti's. They weren't from abroad, which was one good thing, they were buying agents from Milan whose clients are mostly from Scandinavia and England. According to them, they drove down here and arrived at about eleven to meet Moretti at his factory and fix the price of a consignment. After that they wanted to find someone to supply them with majolica, but not artisan work because they wanted a lot of it and they wanted it cheap. Moretti, of course, doesn't deal in glazed ware at all, but since he has a good deal with this agent, and since it was a free day for him, he offered to take them to one or two smallish factories producing low quality stuff in the majolica style, though not the real thing. In fact they went to two places and the agents found what they wanted and placed orders. A little before one o'clock they were at the restaurant. They left towards two and parted company. Moretti, according to his wife, got home before half past two. The family were still sitting round the table, including his brother. They'd finished eating but were drinking coffee and watching the quiz on TV. For what it's worth, the time he came in is confirmed by a neighbour who was there drinking coffee and watching the quiz with them.

'At any rate, while there's no saying that Moretti couldn't have whipped round to the factory between leaving the clients and going home, the girl was dead by then anyway. Look to your left—that's Robiglio's place.'

An impressive pile of concrete and glass with Robiglio's name written large down one side of it and a big car park in front.

'It's big enough . . .'

'He doesn't only supply the industry here,' explained Niccolini, 'he supplies other regions as well, including the tableware factories on the other side of Florence.'

'They don't make tableware here?'

'No, only decorative stuff in terracotta and majolica, and roof and floor tiles too. Nothing in the kitchenware line.'

'Berti told me he was a millionaire . . . Robiglio, I mean.'

'Maybe he was exaggerating, but maybe not.' Niccolini laughed: 'I suppose he told you what they call his house?'

'He did. Is he married?'

'Separated. I don't know much about his wife—before my time—only that as soon as their one daughter was married she moved out. Went back to where she came from —Milan, I think.'

'Then he lives alone in that mansion?'

'Apart from the servants—the joke about the seven lavatories was that there was one for each person in the house, including the servants. Now he's got most of them all to himself. We're almost there so let me finish up on these alibis, such as they are. All Moretti's men got together in the bar at the communist club towards eleven-thirty and hung about there playing cards and chatting until half past twelve when they went to eat at the restaurant. Sestini was the only one who didn't eat there but his house is on the way between the two places and his mates walked with him and saw him go in.'

'If they're telling the truth.'

'If they're telling the truth. Well, that's about it because after that they went back to the club where Sestini joined them again and they played billiards for most of the afternoon.'

When the Marshal made no comment he went on: 'Of course there's nothing to say that somebody else apart from them couldn't have just walked in there . . .'

'No . . .' Again the Marshal had the familiar feeling that something obvious was eluding him, but he could make nothing of it so he remained silent.

'We turn off here. This is the borderline of the pottery area. Further down that road the glass factories start. The old boy lives in splendid isolation down by those orchards there.'

The house, when they reached it at the end of a bumpy lane, was indeed isolated but not at all splendid. It was an austere little bungalow in faded yellow stucco with red clay roof tiles and dark brown shutters. It had been built on the site of a peasant's cottage and the grassy courtyard still had its well in the centre and a dilapidated stone barn which looked as though it had been badly damaged during the war. No doubt it was a very pleasant spot in spring and summer when the surrounding orchards were full of blossom or fruit, but the wintry fields and bare branches along with the overgrown courtyard accentuated the neglected, sad air typical of the house of an old man living alone.

Niccolini rang the bell. As they waited for an answer the Marshal stared at a trailing piece of broken washing line lying in a puddle of yesterday's rain and then at the shutters which no one had opened to let in a little sunshine and air, remembering the years he had passed alone before his wife and children had come up from Sicily. It occurred to him to hope that he didn't live long enough to finish his days alone. A selfish hope which made him feel guilty. Then the door opened and his sadness was dispelled in an instant.

'Come in, come in, you boys! Delighted to see you!' Dr Frasinelli whipped a pipe from his mouth and waved them in, beaming up at them with bright blue eyes in a pixie-like face. He turned and pottered happily along a small corridor to show them into a room on the left, a room as neat and bright as the dapper little man himself, who chatted on as he offered them seats and settled himself in what was evidently his habitual place in front of a booklined wall. 'This used to be my waiting-room when I was in practice—the old surgery's next door, through here . . .'

Here the window and shutters were open and the winter sunshine poured in from the courtyard. The roof of the well was visible and the sweet smell of the doctor's tobacco smoke was pleasant on the clean rainwashed air.

'I gather there's trouble in the town—I hope my pipe doesn't bother you? Young people sometimes find it a bit strong.' He slipped a tobacco pouch from his pocket and kneaded it affectionately. Since neither of them answered his query, bemused at being considered young people, he began to refill his pipe with an air of happy concentration. 'I'm not so well up as I used to be with local gossip since my daughter doesn't come as often as she did. At one time she came every day, insisted on doing a bit of cleaning and cooking for me, though I manage perfectly well by myself, you know what women are. Nowadays she can't manage it, says she's not as young as she was. I have a woman who comes once a week, which is all I need, but she tells me nothing in the way of news, confines herself to recounting the ailments of her whole family, and more especially her own—if I'm to believe half of what she tells me I wonder how she can be on her feet at all but she obviously considers free medical advice to be a perk of the job and intends to make the most of it by cultivating as many illnesses as she can think up. So you'll gather that you'll have to tell me your story from scratch.' He looked from one to the other and sat back in his chair.

The Marshal remained motionless, letting Niccolini take the floor.

'Well, you'll probably think we're as bad as your cleaning woman because we're here looking for advice and information as well. But, to keep it brief, there's been a young Swiss girl found strangled on the sherd ruck outside Moretti's place.'

'That much I heard but I don't know what she was doing there. Did she work for young Moretti?'

'She was working for Berti, learning Majolica, but now and again, when his men were off, she went round to Moretti's place to do a bit of throwing, just to keep her hand in. She wasn't working for him.'

'So you think it's one of Moretti's men?'

'Not necessarily. They weren't working that day and theoretically anyone could have gone in there and, finding her alone . . . The trouble is we're working in the dark and what we need is some background information.'

'On what?'

'Well, I suppose on Moretti, for a start . . .' Niccolini looked a bit embarrassed. 'They say he's a friend of yours.'

The doctor smiled, to himself rather than at Niccolini. 'You could put it that way.'

'It's not that he's a suspect particularly, you understand, less so than anyone since he has a solid alibi, but he's hiding something, even so. Something serious enough to cause a fight with one of his men.'

'Who?'

'Sestini.'

'You mean a quarrel or a real fist fight?'

'I mean a fight. They were going for each other like dogs. And then there are these stories going around about Robiglio, and I'm not happy about his behaviour towards us either. Then when Marshal Guarnaccia here had a word with Moretti's sister—'

'Tina? How is the poor child?' The description seemed apt enough despite Tina's age.

'Half crazy, according to Guarnaccia, and it sounds as though that husband of hers doesn't treat her any too well.'

'Poor creature. So like her mother. And it was she who put you on to Robiglio?'

'Not exactly. I'd heard stories already. In any case, Tina's story was too garbled to mean much, but it did sound as though the Moretti family was connected with Robiglio's dark past and since you were here then . . .'

'I was here.' He took the pipe from his mouth and considered it in silence for a moment. Then he stood up and went over to the open window. With his back to them he said, 'Those were terrible years. I don't say we should forget them, but even so, I don't believe in keeping old hatreds alive. We have to look forward, not back. Are you sure this has something to do with the girl who was murdered?'

'No. We're not sure of anything.'

'What could she have to do with something that happened before she was born?'

'I don't know. I'm being honest with you, I don't know. But I do know that Robiglio's trying to get himself elected. They say he'll try for mayor.'

'I've heard that.'

'And you approve?'

'No. But it's a long time since I mixed myself up in politics. As mayor he might be no worse than another.'

'Perhaps not. But one thing's certain, he won't want his wartime activities advertised just now.'

'No, and I'm the last man to advertise them for a number of reasons, not the least of them being that he was hardly more than a boy then.'

'I understand. But we're not conducting a witch hunt, we're investigating a murder. Whatever you tell us can remain between us unless it turns out that Robiglio's our killer, in which case the elections will hardly be his most immediate problem, and I very much doubt if it will come to that.'

The doctor remained at the window, staring out at the well. At last he turned and said, 'I'm not saying you're wrong in thinking that Morettis are involved with Robiglio, but surely, to cause a young girl to be murdered—is it that you think she found out something?'

'She might have.'

'But what would a foreigner have made of information like that?'

'I couldn't say since we don't know the story.'

'Then take it from me that if this girl became such a danger it could hardly have been because of what happened during the war. It would have had to be something more recent, something more immediately threatening.'

'That's what Guarnaccia here says, but as far as I know, Moretti has nothing to do with Robiglio these days. He doesn't even do business with him.'

'He has done business with him. He once bought a piece of land from him.'

The Marshal who had listened in silence until now spoke quietly.

'Perhaps you could show him the letters.'

'What letters?' The doctor came forward and Niccolini took the package from his pocket and handed it to him. He fished out a pair of reading glasses which he held on the end of his nose like a lorgnette and walked back to the window. 'My eyesight isn't what it should be . . .'

He read through all the letters without comment except for an occasional sigh or grunt of disgust. Then he slapped them back together and handed them over.

'You're right. If things are stirred up to this extent it's better you should know everything.' He settled in his chair and slipped the glasses back into his top pocket with one hand. The Marshal, watching him, noted a slight tremor there. The thin, translucent skin was spotted with brown and the fingers moved with a slow hesitancy as though fumbling in the dark. Only there did the doctor's age show; for the rest, he might have been under seventy. The hands folded slowly over each other and then opened to indicate the window.

'You've seen the well out there? It's dry, has been for years and years, but it came in useful for hiding people during the war. Jews, partisans, and once the parish priest from a village nearby because the SS were looking for him . . . You two are not from these parts I can tell.'

'No,' answered Niccolini, 'I'm a Roman myself and Guarnaccia's from Syracuse.'

'And of course you're very young and don't remember. I don't know whether you realize that half the partisans who died in the fight against nazi-fascism were Tuscans. I'm not making out that our boys were any more dedicated or heroic than others. I suppose they might have been but I'd hesitate to say so. It was just the way things went. The trouble was, you see, that the armistice of '43 was drawn up in such a hurry. So many misunderstandings were never ironed out as they might have been with a bit of thought and patience. Of course, it was inevitable that the Allies didn't trust us. They were frightened of being double-crossed and the result was that they drew up an armistice that eliminated Italy from the list of protagonists of the war, leaving us to deal with the Germans as best we could and going about their business in their own way. It was understandable but it was tragic, as much for them as for us. I said then and I still say that if only there had been some coordination, if only the Allies had made their landing between Rome and La Spezia as they could and should have done, the war would have been over in a matter of weeks instead of dragging on for another year and a half with so many Allied soldiers dead and so many Italian towns destroyed. There need have been no Gothic Line, no bombing in the centre of Florence, none of the so-called German reprisals that wiped out the populations of entire villages for no real military reason.

It was a mistake, and it's been my experience that mistakes result in worse disasters even than deliberate evil intentions do. Even Kesselring himself was frightened when the armistice was signed. In one of Colonel Dollman's letters—I have it here in one of my books but I'll just give you the gist of it—he said that according to Field Marshal Kesselring, if Badoglio had taken command right away and started a large-scale Allied landing near Rome the German defeat would have been inevitable. Well, that's not the way things went. There was no coordination, no unified command and the psychological situation was terrible. After all, to a soldier an armistice means the war's over, willpower and fighting capacity were bound to sag unless a properly established command and rapid battle orders did something to keep them going. As it was, a lot of units found themselves fighting in a vacuum on their own initiative. There were three thousand dead in the first two days. There's no doubt in my mind that the partisans saved the day—not so much because of their attacks on the enemy but because they boosted the morale of the people, gave them something to hope for and restored the will to fight back. In other words, they did unofficially what should have been done officially, and thirty-five thousand of them died doing it.

'Now, be patient with me, Niccolini—Marshal Guarnaccia here is too polite to show it, sitting here without moving a muscle—but I can see you're getting restless, thinking you've come across a real war bore. You'll realize in a moment that that's not the case. If you want to understand these letters you have to understand the way people were feeling and thinking then. Most of the letters are directed against Robiglio and the rest against Moretti and you think the writers are divided into two opposing camps perhaps, but you're wrong. The targets may be different but the motive behind the attacks is the same. That's what you have to understand. It all goes back to what happened one night in this town. A night that changed everything in both

Robiglio's family and Moretti's. You've seen the statue in the square, of course?'

Niccolini stopped sorting and resorting the letters in his hand and looked up.

'The partisan?'

'That's Moretti, the father.'

'It is? But the name . . .'

'Pietro Moro, his *nom de guerre*—though his real name's there, too, if you'll look more closely. He called himself Pietro, but since there were two of them in the brigade who'd chosen the same name, the other boy who was a northerner and very fair-haired became Pietro Biondo and Moretti, who was dark, Pietro Moro.'

'So Moretti's father was a war hero. Well, I didn't know that.'

'For one reason and another it's not talked about, though it's not forgotten. As to the term "war hero", it covers many realities. There were heroes enough of what I call the genuine kind, those who voluntarily sacrificed themselves for others, and Pietro was one of them, or became one of them in the end. But some were just victims of circumstance and others plain fakes—it was amazing how many men declared themselves to have been partisans once the fighting was over, inventing a new past for themselves after having fought in Mussolini's GNR. They just dumped their uniforms after the defeat and found themselves a red neckerchief to come home in. Well, enough of them. Among the genuine partisans there were all sorts, the idealists, the disaffected, the odd character on the run from the law who found it a convenient way to disappear from circulation, and of course the boys who would otherwise have risked being called up to serve Mussolini's new Republic in Salò or packed off to Germany to die in work camps. Moretti, Pietro as you know him, was one of the last group but he had good reasons for being glad to leave his family at that point too. He and young Ernesto Robiglio were both twenty years old that year, but their circumstances were as different as their characters. Robiglio's father was an ardent fascist, and mayor—podestà as it was then—of the town. Young Ernesto was living at home and studying law at the University of Florence. Their factory stood where it stands now, though the present buildings are new since the old place was badly damaged by Allied bombings.

'Moretti—Pietro Moro—was working for his father and uncle in the family business, the same place you know, but in those days they only made field drains and roof tiles. At any rate, young Pietro started work there at age twelve and things went along smoothly enough for a few years until he got involved with his uncle's daughter, Maria, a pretty little thing, small and plump with a mass of curly hair and eyes as large and innocent as a baby's. But she wasn't all there and that's a fact. You could see it in those eyes, pretty and soft but more animal than human . . . You've seen Tina, so you'll understand what I mean. Tina as a child was a replica of her mother, but you've seen how she ended up, and her mother, poor soul, came to an even worse end because of what happened that night.

'By the time she was fifteen Maria was already running after men twice her age and more. Then she took up with Pietro. She was sixteen and he was just seventeen. What made matters worse was their being cousins. I tried to talk him out of it because of that. Too much intermarrying goes on in this town and it's not healthy. I had him in here at the request of his parents and tried to talk some sense into him, basing my arguments on the fact that they were blood relations. I didn't know how much he knew about Maria's behaviour and I was afraid he'd run out on me if I tried to tell him. There's no doubt that he was in love with the girl. In any case, before I could get very far he interrupted me to tell me that I was wasting my breath. The reason he'd let himself be talked into coming to see me was so that he could tell me what Maria had been afraid to come and tell me herself. She was pregnant. Well, you can imagine how things would have gone between the two fathers if they hadn't married. The business was already in severe difficulties because of the war—this was in '41—and a big family quarrel would have meant the end. So Pietro got his own way and married his little Maria. He certainly seemed to have no doubts about the child's being his and I think it probably was. I hadn't seen her hanging around the town since she'd been with Pietro. So they married and moved in with his parents who were living in a corner of the factory. Conditions were cramped and his mother, who had been against the marriage and had been forced to accept it by the men to protect the business, couldn't get on with her daughter-in-law at any price. Things started badly and soon got worse. As their family doctor, I knew a great deal about what was going on but there was little I could do to help, though the mother frequently turned to me for advice—they were communists and so would have nothing to do with the priest—he once went round there claiming that the young people's future was cursed because they hadn't married in church. He was out on his ear within minutes. I tried talking to Maria but it was hopeless. How can you talk about the responsibilities of motherhood to a child? I doubt if her mental age was much above twelve. She was wayward and lazy and did nothing to help her mother-in-law in the house, but what was worse was that within a month of moving in there she began hanging around the men in the factory. Nothing happened, of course. Apart from the presence of the men in the family, including her husband, she was already showing her pregnancy. But it caused violent quarrels, especially between Pietro and his mother, and with all their efforts they couldn't keep Maria under control. Pietro was deeply unhappy and it goes without saying that his mother lost no opportunity of saying "I told you so", as is the way with mothers. When the time came I delivered the baby.'

The doctor paused. Perhaps he was aware of little signs of Niccolini's restlessness. At any rate he smiled and got up from his chair to offer them a glass of vinsanto which he took from a hanging cupboard that had probably once held medicines.

'Have a drop of this, it's particularly good. I no longer drink any myself. One's needs get fewer and fewer with time. No doubt I'll eventually give up eating, too, and then my time will have come.' He chuckled, filling the tiny glasses with care. 'In the meantime I'm very glad to be alive.' He watched them drink, settling down again and refilling his pipe thoughtfully.

'Tina . . . Maria Cristina they christened her, and no brighter than her mother as it turned out—though whatever you may think of the life she leads it's still preferable to being shut in an institution.

'Once relieved of the burden of baby Tina, Maria went back to her old ways and before long Pietro couldn't hold his head up in the town. Up to then the problem had been kept pretty much in the family, as it were, since all she did was hang around ogling the men in the factory. But once the child was born she virtually ignored its existence and started going out. Little Tina was left to the mercies of her grandmother, much to the latter's fury. It even got to the stage where they tried locking her in at nights but night or day made little difference to Maria. Once, on the way back from my rounds on foot, I took a short cut through that orchard down there and found her plumped down in the grass with old Gino Masi, a peasant farmer who was sixty if he was a day. There was no wickedness in the child, she was completely amoral. By '43 there were the German soldiers. You can imagine perhaps why Pietro was eager to join the partisans and escape from what was an impossible situation. He was also in danger of being called up to fight for Mussolini's new Republic. Maria was pregnant again when he left in '44, and for a long time nothing was heard of him. As for Maria . . . well, by that time we had a detachment of twenty or so men of the Wehrmacht stationed up at the villa, most of which they'd taken over for their purpose and, needless to say, Maria found her way up there as often as she could escape the vigilance of her mother-in-law. She understood nothing of the war except that she was often hungry and that her husband had abandoned her. I saw her up at the villa myself many a time.

'The place is a criminal asylum now but in those days it was a mixture of barracks and hospital. We had no hospital here and there was no possibility of transporting the sick in '44. Apart from curfew and restrictions of movement, the Germans had requisitioned everything on wheels. I went up there late mornings and evenings after my rounds. Some of the patients were local emergency cases, but as the Germans retreated towards us from Pisa and from the south the place filled up with their wounded. The villa has seen a lot since the Medici built it. In many ways it's the focal point of the town—you might even say the town wouldn't have come into existence in its present form if the villa hadn't been built. It was the Medici who first brought a group of Spanish monks over here to make Majolica for them—a misnomer that, since it was really Spanish pottery but always imported via Majorca and the name stuck. If it hadn't been for the Medici and that handful of monks who started production up at the villa there wouldn't be the pottery industry that keeps the town going to this day. At any rate, it was from the villa that the Germans held the town under control— though I must say that, apart from their requisitioning, we had less trouble from them than from our local fascists, as vicious a bunch of hooligans as were ever let loose on the world. They cultivated the Germans up at the villa but they got little enough encouragement. The Germans could never quite understand the very personal and parochial nature of Italian fascism. Our local thugs enjoyed strutting about in uniform and contributed little or nothing to the war effort. For the most part the Germans kept out of local disputes and occupied themselves with controlling the town, requisitioning food and trying to defend the railway line and road along the Arno to Pisa.

'At least they fed my patients in the hospital and I could sometimes manage to get a little food or medicine out of them for the more desperate cases on my rounds. That was mostly thanks to the cook, though the sergeant knew well enough that I rarely left the villa empty-handed and turned a blind eye. The cook came of Bavarian peasant stock, built like an ox, Karl his name was. I often wonder what became of him. He always said he wanted to come back here when the war was over but perhaps he didn't even get home alive. Every day, after my hospital round I used to go to the kitchen and there he'd slam a bowl of soup down in front of me and bellow "Eat!" Then he'd pinch my arm and roar with laughter because I was so thin. While I ate he would point around him at all the objects in the kitchen and demand that I tell him their names in Italian. He'd repeat each one after me, frowning so much with the effort that his eyebrows met in the middle. His accent was so thick that he could get nowhere near the right pronunciation but he was always pleased with the results himself. "*Ja, ja!*" he'd bellow with a big grin when he'd managed to get the word out, and then he'd point at another object and the frown of concentration would return. He rarely remembered a word from one day to the next and with each bowl of soup we'd start all over again from scratch. He took little or no interest in the progress of the war, just went on with his job as best he could, waiting for it to be over. Only occasionally, when he'd had a glass of wine too many, he'd get maudlin and start showing me photographs of his wife and children with big tears in his eyes. "In Germany," he'd explain, as though I couldn't possibly know where he came from. Certainly he didn't know why he should be here.

'As for the sergeant, Sergeant Janz his name was, he was always in a temper about something and almost every time I went up there the first thing I'd hear would be his voice howling with rage. The reason could be anything from an Allied bombing raid to a missing button, it was all the same to him, just one more attempt by fate to get at him. He was overweight with blond, almost colourless hair and white skin that burned to a fierce red in the sun. He could work himself up into such a rage that he would swell up like a huge toad and make his eyes pop out. His men were so accustomed to his rages that they never turned a hair, and after a while I got used to him, too. From what I managed to understand, he was a professional soldier and he was furious that a war had come along to disorganize his perfectly orderly life. Only once was there an incident involving him that frightened me. It happened in the summer of '44 when tension was at its highest. Our trouble was that we were right at the outer edge of two fronts, with fighting at Pisa and Leghorn to the west and movement towards Florence to the east and when the Allied advance guard came up the Val d'Elsa, unfortunately for us and for Empoli, too, they deviated to the south of us on one side and to the north of San Miniato on the other. Between that time and our eventual liberation there were terrible reprisals and the incident involving Sergeant Janz could well have been expected to end in a bloodbath. Goodness knows, the provocation was sufficient.

'What happened was that, because of severe communications difficulties caused by the Allied bombings, the Germans had set up a telephone wire connecting them with their Praesidium Command at Signa. It was old Gino Masi—the one I told you I'd surprised in the orchard with Maria—who caused the disaster. I'd seen him that morning, as I often did on my way home, collecting dry brushwood not far from here to store for winter kindling. I remember him pausing and straightening up for a moment to wipe the sweat from under his hat and raise his hand in salute. I'm in an isolated spot up here and it wasn't until the early evening when I set out for the villa that I heard anything. I'd found myself a battered old bicycle by then and as I rode through the central square it was soon obvious that something was up. There wasn't a soul in sight and the silence was so thick it made me think a bomb was about to go off. Every shutter in the square was closed, but when I passed the bar I saw that the metal shutter that rolled down over the doorway was open just a crack at the bottom. I slowed down and got off my bike. I could hear a low murmur of voices inside so I tapped and said who I was, asking what had happened. They wouldn't open up but a woman's voice answered softly that someone had cut the German telephone wires and that partisan activity was suspected. The soldiers from the villa had ordered everyone to stay indoors and were out searching for the break in the wire and the culprits. I pedalled on for a few yards along the empty street, listening to the rattle of my bicycle chain and thinking. As far as I knew, the partisan brigades were fighting further to the south and west of us and an isolated incident like this seemed unlikely. All of a sudden I put the brakes on, almost fell over, turned my bike and began pedalling as fast as I could. A picture had just flashed into my mind of old Masi as I'd seen him that morning. He'd been binding his kindling with wire! It may well be that the thought had half formed itself at the moment I saw him, the thought that he had wire when you couldn't get hold of it at any price in those days. I went on pedalling furiously and the people who were no doubt watching the street through the slats of their closed shutters must have thought someone was dying or that the Germans were after me.

'When I reached old Masi's cottage it was too late. The sergeant was there with four of his men. And someone else was there, too: young Ernesto Robiglio.

'It wouldn't have taken much, of course, to discover who'd cut that wire. Masi's cottage was the only house in the area where they'd found the gap in the wire, and there were the bundles of kindling stacked outside his door in the evening sunshine for all to see. The old man himself was standing in the doorway with four machine-guns pointing at him. I think at that point he still had no idea what he'd done. The sergeant, purple with rage, was screaming at him in German and naturally he didn't understand a word. I stayed at a distance under a peach tree, watching. It seemed inevitable that they would shoot him. I couldn't follow the sergeant's tirade any more than old Masi could, but then young Ernesto spoke up, moving forward and pointing to the wire-bound bundles. I couldn't hear exactly what was said but I saw Masi push back his crumpled hat and scratch his head. He tried to explain himself, opening his big hands to express his ignorance and gazing at the offending bundles in dismay. Then the sergeant began shouting orders and the four soldiers shifted their positions slightly. I thought to myself, "This is it," and half closed my eyes so as not to see him go down, waiting for the burst of fire. There was silence and then another burst of shouting from the sergeant. I opened my eyes properly and saw the sergeant stumping away, still roaring, and his men following. Masi was still in his doorway staring after them, as perplexed as ever. There was no sign of Ernesto. The telephone wire was repaired and nothing further was heard of the incident. Nevertheless, Ernesto's part in it became known and after that people were afraid of him. He was generally to be seen hanging around the Fascio during the day but then I began to see him slinking about after dark, too. I had a pass to be out after curfew because of my work and once or twice I'd seen him racing off in a great hurry on a motorbike. Obviously the Germans up at the villa had disappointed him. Ernesto found the congenial company he was looking for among the SS, as we soon found out.

'The summer wore on, the harvest was got in and promptly requisitioned, the Allies still didn't arrive. Maria was up at the villa more often than she was at home, but since her husband was fighting with the partisans most people held their tongues, at least in front of old Signora Moretti who, poor thing, was saddled with two tiny grandchildren and in danger of losing her only son. If she held her tongue, too, it was because they'd have had little enough to eat if it hadn't been for Maria who never left the villa without a big bagful of food.

'Then one hot night in July, Maria's husband, Pietro Moro, came home.'

'I've often wondered since what would have happened to him if things hadn't gone as they did, and found no answer. Looking back, it seems that things couldn't have gone otherwise, as if all his short life he had been moving step by step towards that inevitable end and that nothing could have prevented it, though God knows I tried that night to save him from himself and what was awaiting him. In this very room.

'I'd seen Maria that day, in fact, as I was toiling up the hill to the villa, pushing my bicycle. She was coming down in a thin flowered frock and broken sandals, carrying an old shopping-bag heavy with food. She smiled and said hello to me, little knowing that not many hours afterwards she was to go up that hill again and that it would be years before she would come down. Long, silent years.

'That night, it was after midnight, I think, though I didn't know the exact hour, I was awakened by what I thought had been a faint scratching at the shutters of my bedroom window. At first I lay still, thinking I'd been mistaken. All I could hear was the sawing of the cicale out there in the hot darkness. Then the faint scratching came again and someone whispered my name. Without lighting the oil lamp on my bedside table, I got up and unlatched the shutters. The window was already open because of the heat. Pietro climbed in and stood there swaying, his face a pale blur in the darkness. I took his arm and led him in here where the blackout was more efficient and I could light a lamp. Even then I had to guide him to a chair and sit him down. I saw some terrible sights during the war but I can't begin to describe to you how the sight of that boy horrified me. He was badly wounded and his torn clothes were soaked in blood, but it wasn't that. It was his eyes. They seemed to be staring back at me from beyond the grave . . . and the truth of it was that they were. Once I'd seen his wounds I took him through there to the surgery where I undressed him. He was carrying a pistol but he refused to give it up. He held it in his hand as I worked, his knuckles showing white through the dirt as he gripped it in pain. I cleaned his wounds as best I could. He'd been hit in four places by machine-gun bullets. One of them was lodged in his groin and I couldn't risk trying to get at it under those conditions. Once he was bandaged up I dressed him in some clothes of mine which once would have been far too tight for him but which hung loosely on him now. He'd had little enough to eat of late by the look of him. I heated up a bowl of ersatz coffee and gave him a piece of the darkish bread which Karl had produced from our grain harvest.

'I began to explain to him that I would willingly have put him in my bed but that the risk of his being found was too great. It occasionally happened that the Germans came to fetch me during the night. He would have to pass the night in the well with straw and a blanket as others had done before him. I would give him something to ease his pain and help him sleep and then wake him at dawn. I promised him that he would be safe there, that the well had saved a good many lives already, and that by dawn I would work out some means of getting him to where he had to go. Up to then he hadn't said a word. Now he spoke.

'"I'm going home."

'"Home? You're mad! Apart from the fact that you'd be caught, think what would happen to your family."

'"I'm going home." His eyes still had that strange, staring look and I think I knew then that I couldn't reach him, that no reasoning could reach him, though I kept on trying.

'"In a matter of weeks the war will be over. If you get caught now—"

'"I'm going home to sleep in my bed with a live warm person next to me. After that I don't care what happens. I just want to sleep in my bed with a live warm body . . ."

'Then he doubled up in his chair and vomited the bread and coffee. I was hoping he'd pass out so that I could keep him here by force, but the staring eyes never closed, barely even blinked. I gave him a little water and tried to get him to take a sleeping pill, but he had all his wits about him and refused it. I doubt now whether it would have put him out, given the strange state of tension he was in. I didn't dare ask him what had happened but it suddenly occurred to me that there might be others of his brigade wandering about in the area, so I risked asking:

'"Did you come here alone?"'

'"Alone . . . yes."'

'"And the rest of your brigade?"'

'"They're dead. Everybody . . . the whole village. All dead. I should be dead, too. We blew up the pontoon bridge. We did it at dawn when it was camouflaged under the river bank because at night they set it up over the river. We did it at dawn. Only one German was killed, just one. I'm thirsty . . ."'

'I gave him the cup of water but he stared down into it without drinking as though he'd already forgotten why I'd given it to him.

'"We couldn't get back to camp in the daylight so we were hidden in a safe house in the village. I don't know who betrayed us . . . maybe they were only guessing, but we'd cut off their retreat and they were half crazy with fear and anger. They came into the village and began shooting everyone on sight, starting with the children who came running out of the houses to see their tanks arriving. They set houses on fire and we could hear women and old people running out screaming with their clothes burning and then the machine-guns. The Germans were shouting 'Partisan! Partisan!'

'"We gave ourselves up, thinking that would stop them, but it made no difference. At the edge of the village there was a stone wall with a steep drop beyond it to a ditch. We were lined up along the wall with our hands on our heads and I could see the ditch was already full of bodies. Behind us the whole village was burning and the people screamed

and screamed . . . I didn't feel afraid, I couldn't feel anything except that it wasn't real. Pietro Biondo was on the
wall next to me and I could hear him moaning as though
he were already hit. Then I felt something burst into me
from behind and we were falling. When I came to there
were no more people screaming but I could still hear German voices shouting and the roar of flames. I could hear
but I couldn't see anything. I was buried under dozens more
bodies. Then I heard Pietro Biondo moaning again exactly
in the same way as before they'd shot us. He wasn't next to
me any more . . . maybe he'd tried to crawl away, but he
hadn't got far, I could still hear him . . . I wanted to tell
him to shut up because if they'd heard him—but I didn't
move or speak. I didn't know how much time had passed,
how long I'd been lying there, but the bodies around me
were cool and I was hot. Then there was silence for hours
but I knew the Germans must still be there because I hadn't
heard the tanks leave. I felt the bodies above me shifting
. . . it was as if somebody was walking over us but there
were no voices. No voices . . . Then I heard the lapping
noise. It was dogs. Starving dogs drinking up the blood.
Much later there was more movement and more orders
shouted. Then I heard jeeps passing along the road that ran
by the wall above. Doors slammed and an Italian voice
shouted. 'The ambulances are here! Is anybody alive?'
  '"Pietro Biondo began moaning again and I sensed a
shifting among the bodies as though he had raised himself.
There was a burst of gunfire and Pietro Biondo stopped
moaning. It was a long time before I heard the tanks leave.
I dragged myself out from under the stiffened bodies. I had
to find Pietro Biondo . . . they'd disarmed us but they'd
done it in a hurry and I knew he had his extra pistol strapped
to his leg. It was going dark and it took me a long time . . .
  '"I followed the ditch until I was away from the village
and then I kept walking. I can feel the wounds more
now . . . than I did then . . ."'
  '"They're stiffening now you've stopped moving." I told

him that there was still a bullet inside him, that I needed to operate, that infection would probably set in.

'"It doesn't matter. I'm tired."

'His eyes . . . they seemed to look right through me. He was lucid enough, to hear him talk, but thinking back on it now I feel that to all intents and purposes he died in that ditch with his comrades. I couldn't stop him leaving.

'I had no hope of getting back to sleep so I sat in here with a book for the rest of the night. It wasn't the Germans up at the villa I was afraid of, it was Ernesto. Less than half an hour after he'd left I heard shots in the distance and I knew it was all over for Pietro.

'It was from his parents that I heard what happened. I don't know where or when Ernesto got on his tracks but it must have been before he reached here because almost the minute he arrived home they burst in on him as though they'd been lurking somewhere around the factory, Ernesto and six men of the SS. When it happened they were all in the kitchen, the parents and Maria in their nightclothes. Pietro had just sat down at the kitchen table and the others were standing round him when the door crashed open. Pietro still had his pistol but before he could fire it they'd shot him. He fell forward with his head on the table and then slid to the floor. The lower part of his face had been shot away but he wasn't dead and his eyes were still open watching them. One of them, Pietro's mother thought he may have been an officer because he was older than the others, came and stood over the boy and said something. Perhaps he was angry at their having had to shoot him like that since it meant they could get nothing out of him. He spotted one of the bandaged wounds and bent to tear open Pietro's clothes. Then he stood back and shot accurately into each wound. That seemed to relieve his feelings. Ignoring the boy's dead body, he demanded wine of the old people and they began to celebrate their catch. Once they'd drunk enough they started on Maria. The parents stood there, pressed back against the kitchen wall. When all six of them had finished with Maria they offered her to young Ernesto. He refused. He had drunk with them and now he vomited all he had drunk on to the kitchen floor. He was clearly terrified by the results of his work and would have liked to run away but didn't dare. They laughed at him and began forcing wine from a flask down his throat.

'Pietro was still lying on the floor in a pool of blood which had sprayed the white wall behind him. When they were ready to leave they picked up the body and loaded it on to the back of their jeep. Maria was lying dazed on the kitchen table where they had left her among broken glasses and spilled wine, too terrified even to cover herself. They came back for her, dragging her to her feet, and took her away with them. The two children, thank God, had slept through it all in the next room.

'All this I heard later from the old people. The first direct news I had was the following morning when one of the sergeant's men from the villa came hammering at my door. I was still in here, fully dressed, though I must have fallen asleep towards dawn and his knocking woke me.

' "Come!" He had left the engine of his motorbike running.

'Although it was early the sun was already hot. We had to pass through the square and I saw little groups of people huddled around the edge of it in the shadows staring in silence at what looked like a heap of rags lying in the centre with a cardboard notice placed on it. The notice said "Partisan" in big red letters. The heap of rags was what was left of Pietro Moro.

'Seeing that he was dead and knowing nothing, I didn't connect my being called to the villa with the happenings of the night before. Nevertheless, when I saw the sergeant I tried to tell him that Pietro's body should be removed and given to his parents for burial. The sergeant shook his head and raised three fingers. He couldn't speak much Italian but he understood me if I spoke slowly. For my part I understood only too well what the three fingers meant. The same thing had happened often enough elsewhere. Pietro's body was to be exposed with that label on it for three days as a warning.

'"SS," the sergeant said. "Go away. Maybe come back—kaputt! Everybody!"

'"You mean if we bury him . . .?"

'"Kaputt! Kaputt!"

'For once he was not in a temper. He looked as if he'd been up all night. Certainly he hadn't shaved and his uniform was sweated and crumpled. I'd never seen him like that before.

'He beat his chest with a thick fist: "Nothing can do. SS!"

'"I understand." I began to think he'd sent for me to warn me against burying Pietro. He often used me as interpreter for the town since I was the person he saw most often. But then he said, "Come."

'They showed me Maria. She was on a small truckle-bed which they'd set up in a linen room. Seeing the bloodstained sheet I thought at first she was dead, though her face was uncovered, but when I approached her she opened her doe-like eyes. She didn't recognize me. She never recognized anyone again. I did what I could for her but I didn't think she'd live. I won't go into detail. Suffice it to say that they must have tortured her for most of the night. In the end they had cut off part of her tongue. The child couldn't have told them anything. She knew nothing of her husband's partisan activities.

'For a while I attended her every day. Although she never spoke or recognized me there was some slight improvement in her physical condition. I was worried about her feet. There were some broken bones which needed much more specialized attention than I could offer and little hope, in that period of turmoil, of getting it. The poor child never cried or protested when I was dressing her wounds, just watched me with her big soft eyes. It was as if she had exhausted her capacity for reacting to pain. Sometimes, when I had finished, I would turn to find Karl standing in the doorway of the tiny room with a bowl of soup in his hands, his eyebrows meeting in the middle with distress.

'Then the Allies arrived. First their aeroplanes stopped dropping bombs and began dropping leaflets telling us to remove obstructions from the streets and indicate the position of mines to the advance patrols, and to hide our food stocks from the retreating enemy—as if we still had any! The villa was abandoned by the Wehrmacht and the hospital beds there filled up with wounded Americans. I no longer went there, being fully occupied with an outbreak of typhoid near here. Before too long I had typhoid myself and was put into hospital quite a way away from here. At the time I thought it a great misfortune indeed to have survived a war only to succumb to an illness caught from my patients. But it's an ill wind . . . I recovered and married one of my nurses from that hospital, the best day's work I ever did in my life, God rest her soul.

'This house had been damaged when the Allies passed through and for the time being we lived with her parents until I could afford to rebuild. Doctors were in short supply everywhere and I had no difficulty in finding work to do. In the end it was five years before I rebuilt and went back into practice here. That would have been the spring of 1950.

'By that time the villa was in an odd transitional stage. There were a few mental patients up there and a number of old people who had nothing particularly wrong with them but who had nowhere to go or no one to care for them. There was a doctor in residence, so I had no reason to go up there until that summer when he telephoned me and introduced himself, asking me to come to the villa as he would like my opinion on one of the inmates. Oddly enough, it was when I was on my way up there for the first time that I met old Signora Moretti. She was shopping in the piazza in the early evening and there was a little girl with her, about eight years old or so and the image of Maria. I stopped the car to speak to them and having patted the little Tina on the head I naturally asked after her mother. Signora Moretti gave the child a push.

'"Go and get in the queue at the greengrocer's."

'Once the child had gone she looked at me tight-lipped.
'"Tina knows nothing about her mother and doesn't need to."
'"Then Maria died? I didn't know."
'"It would have been better for all concerned if she had died that night."
'"Then she's still up there . . ." Could that be why I'd been sent for?
'Signora Moretti pointed to the newly-erected bronze statue in the square at my back.
'"If it hadn't been for that girl I'd have had a son to comfort my old age, not a statue and two orphaned grandchildren. My boy would never have gone off if she hadn't behaved the way she did. That one got what she asked for and whether she lives or dies is all the same to me. I've told them up there and I'll tell you the same. No German sets foot in my home ever again. Let God forgive them because I never will!"
'I went on my way, thinking, as is only natural, of that terrible night and of Signora Moretti who had seen her son slaughtered in her own kitchen, wondering if that sort of wound could ever heal. I understood her bitterness well enough, but it wasn't until I reached the top of the hill and entered the gardens of the villa that I understood the true implication of her words.'

CHAPTER 7

'I parked my car outside the main gates and began walking up the drive, looking up at the balustrade along the top of the villa with its terracotta urns outlined against the blue sky. The ochre façade of the building was a little weathered but the war had left it untouched, and the dark cypresses at each side were still and tipped with a rosy golden light in the evening sunshine. I've always found comfort in the presence of beautiful old buildings that have survived through the centuries. The war which was such a huge event in my life was a short-lived triviality among many others that the villa had lived through. On either side of me lay a formal garden with worn statues standing among the orderly low hedges and shaven lawns, and tiny birds were chirping as they hopped about looking for their evening meal.

'In front of the main doors of the villa there's a wide gravelled space with huge red plant pots around it. At that time of year they were spilling over with flowers, mostly huge red geraniums, but there were two lemon trees and I paused to enjoy their perfume. I'm fond of plants and when my wife was alive the courtyard out there was a mass of flowers . . .

'Only when I stopped did I notice a tiny figure working behind one of the big red pots. A little boy, he didn't look more than three years old, was plucking deadheads from a geranium and dropping them into a bucket. He had pale golden-red hair that bobbed about in the sunlight as he worked and I was amazed to see such dexterity in so tiny a child. He looked up when he heard my footsteps and I smiled at him. He didn't smile back, just stared at me with a pale serious face. He was an ugly enough little thing apart from his hair, and I must say I was disconcerted by his expression, which was anything but childlike. Nevertheless, I spoke to him as one does automatically to a child.

'"That's a big bucket for a small boy."

'He stared at me and then at the bucket, frowning. Then he dropped another deadhead into it and stood waiting, without looking at me, to hear what I would say next.

'"Are you helping your daddy?" I thought he was probably a gardener's child.

'"No." At any rate this remark seemed to have gone down better and had warranted an answer. This time I decided it was my turn to wait. He stood there opening and closing his fist with a dead flower inside it and I looked about me, breathing in the perfume of the lemons while he considered. Then he said: "Helping Giuseppe."

"'Is Giuseppe the gardener?"

"'Yes. Then I have to help the doctor and then Tanza."

'I was more puzzled than ever. This could hardly be a three-year-old despite his size.

"'You help a lot of people. How old are you?"

"'Five and I had a cake and Tanza made it and the doctor put candles." He said it all in one breath, staring up at me earnestly. No sign of a smile. The cake was obviously as serious a business as his helping.

"'I'm fond of cake myself, and of flowers, too. Those are lovely geraniums."

'He didn't answer me. I lit a pipe and stood watching him until he had finished the plant he was working on and there wasn't a sound except the chirping of the birds and the shuffle of his little shoes on the gravel. After a moment he began dragging the metal bucket away—he wasn't tall enough to lift it and I must say I wouldn't have dared offer to help him. When he had disappeared from view I headed for the main doors and saw that they were open. A young man I didn't know but guessed must be the resident doctor was standing in the doorway.

"'Good evening, Dr Frasinelli? I see you've already met my problem patient."

"'The little boy?" I shook hands with him and I must say I was puzzled. "He's a patient here?"

"'In a manner of speaking—but I thought you knew ... He was born here and since I was told you attended his mother I imagined you'd have heard about him."

"'His mother ...? But who—you don't mean Maria ...?"

"'That's right. A sad case, if ever there was one. Then you didn't know? I'm afraid I've given you a shock. Shall we go into my office and talk about it?"

'I followed him without a word. It *was* a shock, though I couldn't have explained exactly why. It was true that when doing what little I could for the wreck that had been Maria, this was the one possibility I hadn't taken into consideration, though logically I should have done. I hardly expected her to live, of course, and in the chaos of those days there was hardly time to think of extraneous possibilities, one just struggled along from day to day. But more than anything, as we settled into the doctor's office, the words of Signora Moretti began to take on a new and clearer meaning. "I've told them up there . . . no German will ever set foot . . ." They weren't the random words I had thought, she was talking about the tiny boy with red-gold hair, a living reminder of that dreadful night.

'I pulled myself together.

'"I'm sorry. Yes, you did give me a shock. Any reminder of that night . . . I suppose this child is . . ."

'"So it would seem from the date of his birth."

'"My God!"

'"He's not unique, you know."

'"I suppose not. It must be true, then, as he said, that he's five now."

'"Five and three months."

'"He's very small."

'"It's a wonder he's alive at all. His mother couldn't feed him. She's never really been aware of his existence. The poor little chap fared badly at first but he's a survivor, and bright enough, too, though of course he isn't developing normally as one can only expect in a place like this."

'"Who looks after him?"

'"Everybody and nobody. He spends most of his time with Costanza, the cook."

'"The one he calls Tanza?"

'"That's right."

'"Then that's why . . . it was the first thing I noticed about him, that he looked at me with the eyes of an adult."

'"He's never seen another child."

'"My God! But couldn't you have—"

'"Couldn't I have what? He shouldn't be here, that's obvious. His position here is anomalous and I for one have been unable to make sense of the bureaucratic knot that would have to be untangled to get him out of here. If I should ever manage it what do you think would happen to him? Another institution where he'd be lost among hundreds of others and probably wouldn't survive. He'd certainly never get out and he'd have little hope of growing up normally."

" "Then surely adoption . . . "

" "Adoption? Even if it weren't too late—people want brand-new babies when they adopt, they don't want sickly undergrown five-year-olds, among other things his heart is weak—not to mention the red tape involved with his mother alive but unable to give her permission. Besides which, you tell me who would want the child of an SS rapist and a woman in a mental asylum."

" "You're right, of course. I apologize. You must have already tried."

" "I've tried."

" "The sins of the fathers . . . I always hated that idea but when you think about it in concrete terms it isn't a moral condemnation, just an observation of the fact. Poor little fellow. What's to be done?"

" "I was hoping you could help."

" "In what way?"

" "As I said, he's never seen another child, but he has a half-brother and sister."

" "You mean . . .? But they're the last people who'd want him!"

" "They're the only people, his only hope. They're legally his family."

" "He has their name?"

" "He's registered as Filippo Moretti. We all know that he's not the son of the young partisan who was shot but that's whose son he's registered as, since he was Maria's husband."

" "And you seriously expect Maria's in-laws to take him in? After what happened?"

'"He could go to them without any red tape. They don't even need to adopt him, they can take him in. Legally he's their grandchild."

'"They'd never do it! I saw Signora Moretti on my way here and it may be that she already suspects something of the sort. She'd never do it."

'"There's nobody else."

'"What about Maria's parents?"

'"They're dead. They were among the last victims of the typhoid epidemic at the end of the war."

'"Then Moretti's running the factory single-handed?"

'"I suppose so. The Morettis are his only hope. You know them, you could help."

'"I hope you're right. Perhaps, given time, they might come round."

'"There is no time."

'"But if he's already been here five years, surely—"

'"There is no time. Within six months this place is to become a criminal asylum. The geriatric and mental patients will be moved out within three months, in time for the workmen to complete the necessary alterations. I'm in the middle of tackling that bureaucratic knot I mentioned. I've already found a possible place for little Moretti in an orphanage. I don't want to send him there."

'"I understand. It's become a personal matter with you. You're fond of the child."

'"Yes, though it's something more than that. I admire his will to survive. I can't explain myself completely—it's not the way one is normally fond of a child. I find it difficult even to think of him as a child, to be honest, but you'll understand when you know him better."'

'Well, he was right. Over the next few weeks I began to get to know little Moretti and to feel a strange sort of affection for him. He was an odd little creature and he took some getting used to, but there was something about him, a fierce way of living as hard as he could despite his unusual and confined life. Whatever time of day I called up there he was always busy "helping" someone or other, and before long he was "helping" me, too. It had occurred to me to take him with me in the car on my evening visits so that at least he could see a little of the world outside the villa and the best way of presenting the idea to him without frightening him seemed to be to ask him to "help" me.

'I'll never forget our first outing. All the way down the hill in the car he was silent, and when I glanced sideways I saw his tiny hands clutching the dashboard, the knuckles white with strain. When he got out he walked very close to me but without allowing me to hold his hand. I didn't make any comments or point anything out to him, just kept a close watch on him. His thin face was set in a determined frown and his body was trembling, but he clutched valiantly on to a small old leather bag which I'd brought along for him to carry. I couldn't give him my real bag which I knew was far too heavy for him but I had realized by then that as long as he was "helping" he felt secure.

'We were only out for about an hour and a half and on most of the visits he waited for me in the car. Nevertheless, at the end of it I could see that he was exhausted with the strain. Only once did he pause to show an interest in something on his own initiative. We were passing the church of Santo Stefano and the doors were wide open. Perhaps there was to be a benediction but at the moment there was no service going on. Glowing in the semi-darkness at the far end of the left aisle there was a big bank of candles, and that was what had arrested his attention. I stopped beside him and waited, not saying anything. Very quietly, and without being able to put in more than two or three of the words he began to sing "Happy birthday to you", staring at the candles, his eyes bright but his expression as solemn as ever.

'After a few trips he got used to the car and the busy streets, but it was never more than a spectacle for him, I think. His real world was the villa and its inmates, and even when he saw other children around he made no connection between them and himself. I remember once I'd left him in the car while visiting an old lady on the Via Gramsci and when I came out I noticed he was gazing very hard at something, almost with his nose pressed to the glass. I followed his glance and saw that he was watching a group of mothers and children in a little amusement park across the street. It's not much more than a bit of grass with a couple of benches and a roundabout, but his taking an interest in it seemed a good sign so I suggested going across to take a closer look. He came along without a word and stood looking in over the low hedge surrounding the grass.

' "Do you want to go in?"

'He shook his head but seemed quite pleased to go on watching. It was only then that I noticed his half-brother and sister were there, playing on the roundabout. I looked about and spotted old Signora Moretti. She saw me, too, all right, but turned her head away. We stood there for a while and I was half hoping that she might come over or at least acknowledge our presence, but she didn't. I observed her two grandchildren. I knew little of them, since the family hadn't come back to me as patients on my return to the town. The boy—Beppe he was called, though I didn't know his name at the time—was slow and heavy and rather uncoordinated in his movements. Tina was overdeveloped for her age and looked too much like Maria for comfort. I looked down at little Moretti with his fierce thin face and intelligent adult eyes, and it occurred to me then that perhaps they needed him as much if not more than he needed them. And in that I turned out to be right. He stood back from the low hedge, frowning.

' "I have to go."

' "Don't you like it here?"

' "I have to help Tanza."

'He always knew what time it was, as if by instinct. It was almost six and at that hour he always went to the kitchen to help Costanza prepare supper for the patients.

'As we drove away I was thinking hard. I felt I'd found a talking point, at least as far as old Moretti was concerned, but as long as his wife was blocking my way I knew I wouldn't get anywhere. I'd already been to see them, of course, but I'd got nowhere. Old Moretti, though he felt the loss of his only son, was less bitter about it, more philosophical, you might say. "What's done is done," was more or less his attitude and he had nothing against the child. But he knew how his wife felt and he had no intention of helping my cause at the risk of provoking trouble with her. I couldn't blame him. I couldn't blame her, either, that she'd set herself against me. In a brief outburst of anger during my attempt at talking her round she had let it out that one of the SS men who had been there that night had reddish hair like the child's. Perhaps she felt she was getting some revenge, who knows?

'At any rate, what I felt as we drove back to the villa that day was that I would only get somewhere if something happened to unblock the situation. I needed a piece of luck. I suppose you could say that I got it, though it wasn't what I'd expected and certainly not what I was hoping for. Just over two weeks later, Signora Moretti died of a stroke.

'I had to move quickly because time was running out. As soon after the funeral as could be considered decent I went to see Moretti. He knew why, of course. What he didn't know was that I'd been doing some quiet investigating in the meantime and had an ace up my sleeve.

' "Is it about that child?"

' "It's about all three of the children, and about yourself. How long do you think you can go on running your business single-handed?"

' "I'm not of retiring age yet."

' "But you soon will be. Who's going to take over? Your brother had no other children besides Maria so I suppose there's nobody on that side?"

' "I have my grandson."

'I didn't say anything, just looked at him. I hadn't been

far wrong in my estimate of his grandson's capabilities and in the uncomfortable silence that followed he scratched his head and looked about him at the ramshackle factory, frowning.

'"He'll learn. He'll have to learn. He's a willing lad and I have some good reliable workmen he'll be able to depend on."

'"If they're willing to work for him."

'"They'll have to. He's my heir when all's said and done."

'"He's one of your heirs."

'"Oh, Tina . . ."

'"I wasn't thinking of Tina."

'"You mean that child at the villa? He's not my son's child, you know that."

'"I know it. But you might have difficulty proving it in court. He's registered as a Moretti."

'"My boy was already dead when those bastards . . . what do you mean— in court?"

'"I mean when he claims a third of your property on your death."

'"He can't do that!"

'"He can. But then he hardly needs to. He already owns half of this factory, the half you calmly took over when your brother, Maria's father, died."

'Moretti's face was green. I don't know to this day whether he was pretending ignorance and knew what the situation was and thought he'd get away with it, or whether he'd acted in good faith. I'm inclined to think the latter, judging by his bewilderment.

'"But Maria was crazy, I never thought . . ."

'"Well, start thinking now. That child owns half your business and when you die he'll own more than half. He's also the only person likely to be capable of running it and so providing for your other two grandchildren who are not. Think it over, Moretti, and give me your answer by the end of this week."

'"My answer . . .?"

' "That's right. At the moment the child needs a home. I advise you to give him a home with you and let him grow up with his half-brother and sister. That way, when the time comes . . . you understand me?"

'I left him stunned. Nevertheless, by the end of the week he'd set things in motion and in a very short time little Moretti was received into his family with no ceremony. I drove him down there from the villa. It reminded me of the first time I'd taken him out; he was white and rigid and I knew he was trembling. That weak little heart must have been beating fit to burst but he didn't say a word or shed a tear. I left him standing in the kitchen, that same kitchen where, in a welter of blood and wine, fear and chaos, his frail life had been conceived. There was no one there to receive him. It was twelve o'clock and the two children were still at school. The wife of one of Moretti's workmen who lived nearby came in each day to get lunch for them and then do a bit of housework but she hadn't arrived yet. Moretti himself was busy in the factory. I had my rounds to finish, so I had no choice but to leave him there. The last I saw of him he was sitting waiting on a kitchen chair with his short thin legs dangling, his face chalk white and expressionless, clutching a small brown paper parcel containing his few spare clothes.

'I didn't sleep much that night, I can promise you. I couldn't help imagining my own little girl in his place . . .

'Only now that I had succeeded did I wonder if I'd been right to interfere. It was my wife who calmed me down, pointing out that the alternative would have been an orphanage. She was right, of course, but even so I didn't sleep. I kept seeing him sitting there alone, and wondering what was going through that strange, half adult mind of his.

'I didn't see him again for some time. The next news I had of him was from the woman who went in to help. I was relieved to find that she was beginning to take to him.

' "An odd creature and no mistake," she said, "but he's a worker, I'll say that for him. I call him my little helper.

He's taken to looking after the other two—who, between you and me, aren't as they should be—like a mixture of guard dog and nanny. It's a comical sight, I can tell you, him so small and the other two such big lolloping creatures as helpless as the day they were born. Just like their mother, crazy Maria—she died, did you hear? Only a few days after they moved her from the villa. Shock, if you ask me, after all those years."

'Well, I might have expected that that's the way things would go, knowing little Moretti as I did. Unfortunately, things went very differently at school. I saw him one day in the playground as I was passing by. He was standing back against the school wall, alone, watching the others run about, just as he'd watched them that day at the park. He looked a forlorn figure but it may be that he wasn't unhappy. He didn't know how to play, and perhaps it was too late for him to learn. I decided that next time I passed I would try and find time to make inquiries of his teacher.

'When I did the news wasn't good. It seemed he was considered a disruptive influence. This came as a surprise, I must say. I had expected her to say he was withdrawn, that he didn't mix with the others and so on, but not this. However, the child was so completely detached from the group that often, when she was teaching, he would get up and wander off to stare out of the window or to try to leave the classroom altogether. It was obvious that he meant no harm, but he was completely uncontrollable and naturally the other children used him as a welcome distraction. He was learning nothing and evidently the teacher considered him subnormal and would have been glad to be rid of him. I asked her if he was bullied by the other children, given that he was so small for his age. The question seemed to embarrass her. There had been a number of incidents in the playground.

'"They'd found out who he was, you see . . ."

'"What do you mean, who he was?"

'"That he was a German. At first they just stood around

him chanting at him, then they took to hitting him. He didn't react or defend himself and he didn't tell anyone."

'"He didn't tell anyone? But there must have been an attendant on duty."

'That seemed to be at the root of her embarrassment. All she said was: "There are a lot of people around here who have no use for Germans."

'"So it was allowed to go on? When did you find out?"

'"When an attendant came to complain about Moretti's older brother—half-brother, I should say. He'd beaten up two boys. It turned out that they'd been attacking his brother. The attendant couldn't stop him and had to call for help. Big Beppe, as everybody calls him, is enormous for his age and as strong as an ox but he's slow and usually docile and never causes trouble. Nevertheless, he was half crazy with anger and the attendant was terrified."

'"Well, at least that probably put a stop to their tormenting little Moretti."

'"I imagine so. But in one way or another the child is always causing trouble and he learns nothing here."

'I confess that in a way I was pleased at the idea of Moretti's being defended by his great brute of a half-brother. At least it meant he'd become part of the family. But there's no doubt that over the years it's always been Moretti who's defended him. He's a poor slow-witted creature and people have always teased him. They can make him believe anything and are always ready to get a cheap laugh at his expense.

'It was disappointing, though, to hear that little Moretti was learning nothing at school because I was convinced that he was bright, brighter than average.

'It wasn't long before he learned one thing, that he could stay off school fairly often and get away with it. The old man took little notice and would sign his absence book without making much fuss.

'The following year things improved slightly. His new teacher took a bit more interest in little Moretti's case and discovered that the child was something of a genius at mathematics. He whipped through the year's textbook in a couple of months and after that it was a job to give him enough to do. There was little improvement in other respects, though, and when obligatory school came to an end for little Moretti, he left only just literate and without a diploma, to start work in the factory.

'There's no doubt that theoretically at least he's wasted there, but he doesn't know it and he's never been dissatisfied with his lot, which counts for much in this life. That brief moment of glory when his intelligence suddenly manifested itself through his brilliance in mathematics is probably just a dim memory for him, if he remembers it at all. His character has never changed from the first day I saw him working busily at a geranium plant with a frown of concentration on his face. Once in the factory he threw all his considerable energy into becoming a skilled potter and when the old man retired he was ready not just to take over the business but to expand it. He began producing garden pots as well as tiles and drains, and it wasn't long before that side had developed to such an extent that it took over completely. He exports all over Europe from that tumbledown place of his. I often wonder what he might have become in different circumstances . . .

'All his remaining energies went into looking after his cumbersome brother and sister—not that the brother's ever been a trouble to him; he's not capable of helping to run the business, as I'd known he wouldn't be, but he works night and day, doing all the heaviest jobs. Poor Tina was more of a problem. She's given him a lot of worry over the years, but he'd defend both of them to the death, like a ferocious guard dog, as that teacher once said. He married —I suppose you know that—but in typical fashion he married a girl from an orphanage who hadn't a soul in the world or a penny to her name. Someone else for him to look after, to help. That's little Moretti all over. It seems to have turned out all right, though, and they have a little girl. As soon as he could afford it, he took a flat in town and ceased living in the factory. It's not a big flat, I believe, but he told me there'd always be a room in it for his brother—Tina was with the nuns then—and I wondered how his young wife would take that because Big Beppe's not everyone's idea of what you want about the home, but I gather he spends ninety per cent of his time holed up in the factory, not bothering anybody. It's been something of a standing joke in the town, ever since he got Tina off, whether he'd find a willing bride for his poor half-witted brother but it hasn't happened yet.

'Here I am rambling on and I've completely forgotten to tell you about Robiglio, who is of more interest to you, I suppose, than all this family gossip. Needless to say he vanished after that night when Pietro Moro was killed. I assume he went north and I found out later that he'd been called up to serve in the GNR shortly afterwards. As the Allies got threateningly close to us his father went north, too, and at the end of the war succeeded in crossing the border to Switzerland, which is more than Mussolini managed to do—but then, he was a slippery character, old Robiglio, much more so than his son ever managed to be. As I say, young Ernesto vanished after that night and the Robiglio factory and house, both damaged by bombings, remained deserted for years. Then, in the early 'sixties, I had a letter from him. It didn't come as a great surprise to me, I might say, though I was surprised at its promptitude which could only mean that he was well informed on everything that was happening here. The letter, you see, arrived within a month of old Moretti's death. The only two eyewitnesses of his treachery were out of the way and he wanted to come back and set up in business again. The only obstacle, as he saw it, was me. He knew well enough that I'd followed his activities during the war. I'd seen him so often slinking about after curfew up to no good and he was afraid of me. I didn't come to a decision without long thought, and when I did I made what you might think a strange request of him. I asked him for what was to all intents and purposes a confession, that is, I asked him to write to me giving a full account of the events of that night, including his own part in them, at the same time giving him my assurance that I had no intention of openly denouncing him. Don't misunderstand me, I had no intention of blackmailing him and I told him so. My feeling was that there'd been enough bloodshed and anger in the past, enough bitter reprisals following the war. Nevertheless, if Ernesto came back I knew that in a short time, with the means at his disposal, he'd be in a position of power in the town and at that point he'd only to wait for my death and he could proclaim himself a saint with nobody in a position to oppose him. That idea stuck in my gullet. Maybe I'd no right to do what I did but I'm glad I did it, and if he gets himself elected mayor, even more so. I may not live as long as he does but that letter will, and he has no means of knowing whose hands it will be put into when I'm gone. I don't say it keeps him on the strait and narrow path altogether but it will make him careful of doing any more damage in this town.

'Well, there it is. He came back, rebuilt his factory and house and married. His old father's long dead, of course.

'For years I've observed them, Ernesto Robiglio and little Moretti, as they worked and planned and gained acceptance in the town. Moretti gained it unconsciously, keeping himself to himself, doing a good job and paying a fair wage, looking after his family and doing no harm to anyone. Robiglio did it consciously, with his money. I wondered more than once if their paths would ever cross. Nobody, by the way, has ever set eyes on that letter other than myself. Moretti knows about it. When the old man died and he took over the factory I had him up here and told him the truth about his birth. I also told him about the letter when it arrived. I felt he had a right to that.

'And now I suppose I must tell you the truth about this business of the land that he bought from Robiglio as Tina's dowry. I'm trying to be fair. Young Moretti means a lot to me, you'll have understood that, I'm sure, but I'm not making him out to be a saint and I'd rather you knew the truth of it than imagined worse.

'In the first place, whatever people say, the idea for that deal over the land and Tina didn't originate with Moretti but with the crafty old so-and-so who married her. Moretti was in a tight spot all right; he didn't want his sister put in an asylum and he could hardly take her in at home. Even apart from her behaviour, there was the fact that they were expecting their child by then and there wasn't room. It was ironic that he should find himself in the situation I'd once been in when looking for a home for him. At any rate, he came to see me and told me the whole story, the suggestion of this land-hungry peasant that he should buy a piece of land on the cheap from Robiglio as a dowry on the grounds that, according to the peasant, Robiglio "owed him a favour"— Moretti, that is. At the centre of all this was the letter. The peasant didn't know about it, he only knew the story and that from hearsay, but Moretti knew and he came and asked me for it.

'I refused. I felt for him and I told him so but I refused. I said that if he felt it was the right solution he could try and convince Robiglio to sell, anyway, without being devious about it.

'"I can't afford to buy. I'm in debt over the apartment and I've just taken on a new thrower. Then there's a child on the way."

'"I can't help you, not that way. It would be blackmail."

'"In a good cause."

'"But still blackmail."

'"From what you told me it's no more than he deserves!"

'"I won't do it, Moretti."

'"Then why did you ever want that letter if you won't use it?"

'"To keep Robiglio from doing more harm, not to harm him."

'"You know what will happen to Tina?"

'"I won't do it. Go to Robiglio. Tell him you want that
land and why. Ask him to let you pay in small instalments.
He can only say no. Always try the simplest way first. I'm
not saying it will work. If he's anything like his father he
has no conscience, which is why I invented one for him and
keep it locked in a drawer. Even so, try it. As to his owing
you a favour, it's true that you probably owe your very
existence in this world to him. Whether you look on that as
a debt he owes you or one you owe him is for you to decide.
If it doesn't work, send that old rascal who wants Tina to
me and we'll see if we can't appease him with a promise of
something later on when you can afford it. But I warn you
of one thing: don't try putting pressure on Robiglio by
pretending you can get your hands on that letter because
he'll immediately check with me and I'll deny it."

'Well, whatever he told Robiglio it seems to have worked.
He got the piece of land on deferred payment. Although I'd
suggested it myself, nobody was more surprised than I was
that it worked, and to be absolutely honest with you I had
a moment of doubt about how Moretti had managed it. So
much so that I made a telephone call to Robiglio. I wanted
to be sure that there had been no false menaces concerning
that letter. Robiglio assured me that it hadn't been mentioned.

'"We came to an amicable agreement."

'It was none of my business to insist on knowing the terms
of their amicable agreement if it didn't concern me or the
letter, so I had to let it go at that. What other people may
think their terms were I don't know. Probably they don't
know either. The point about these anonymous letters, as
I've already said, is that they're all aimed at the same thing,
Nazi-fascism. For those people Robiglio is the son of his
father and Moretti the son of his. Racial hatred is like a
volcano. The flames of the great eruption of the last war
may have died down but the volcano goes on smouldering.
Nothing has changed. It only needs an excuse, economic
depression, threatened vested interest, whatever you will,

and it's ready to erupt all over again. Now you've seen it for yourselves in microcosm in this small town. As long as things are peaceful we're hospitable and polite to the German buyers who come to buy our pottery and the German tourists who rent our country cottages. But now a girl has been murdered and the old flames have been fanned.

'I don't envy you your job, I can tell you. I hope I've made it easier for you by telling you the truth of what's behind these anonymous letters, if only so that you can eliminate the irrelevant. I can't do more than that. I don't know who this Swiss girl was and I don't know what's going on between Moretti and Robiglio now. I can only promise you that just as I refused to give Moretti that letter years ago to help him settle Tina, I refused just as firmly to give it to him yesterday in this very room. I don't know why he wants it now, he wouldn't tell me, though I did my best to find out. Perhaps you have some idea yourselves. Isn't that what brought you here?'

CHAPTER 8

The car was crashing over potholes in the lane which hadn't seemed to be there when they came down it. Niccolini was driving too fast.

'I'm driving too fast . . . damn! Sorry.'

A tractor tried to pull out from an orchard to their right.

'Eh, no!' He leaned on his horn, 'Back you go, laddie, we're in a hurry!'

Perhaps he couldn't have said why they were in a hurry if anyone had asked him. Nobody asked him, certainly not the Marshal who sat silent and uneasy behind his dark glasses, but he didn't complain even when he was bounced out of his seat, and for once he was glad of Niccolini's ebullient activity which tended to relieve his feelings. Not a word had passed between them yet about what they had

heard but he knew by unspoken agreement they were head-
ing for Moretti's place and that there was no time to lose.
They might have been trying to prevent a murder rather
than investigating one.

'Blast these lights . . . they're going to be red—I knew
it!'

The car didn't quite stop but braked and continued edging
forward inch by inch. The Marshal, who was feeling slow
and heavy, incapable of logical action, observed the big boot
toying with the accelerator and the gloved hand that tapped
the steering-wheel impatiently and thought to himself:
Thank God he's in charge, somebody wide awake and
efficient who can take some sort of decision, put some facts
together. As for himself, his head was full of moving images,
some of them first-hand, some of them inspired by the
doctor's story, and all of them slowing down and slowing
down until they became silent tableaux. An ugly little boy
reaching for a dead geranium head in a lemon-scented
garden. Maria spreadeagled on the kitchen table, a pale,
watching face at the window of the house with the seven
lavatories, Berti creeping out from the dark cavern of a kiln,
thin and grey, crawling out over the crumbled brickwork at
the kiln's mouth. Berti's thin fingers spinning his hair-fine
brush that made patterns appear like magic. Why Berti?
What was the point of thinking about him, if you could call
it thinking? It was Moretti who mattered, Moretti towards
whom they were racing as the lights changed and the car
leapt forward, throwing him back in his seat. Moretti
who . . . Were they going to arrest him, or to protect him?
Perhaps it was time they called the Captain. It was all very
well to collect a lot of miscellaneous information, but you
needed someone with brains to make some sense of it all.
In the meantime, at least there was Niccolini who would
act instead of sitting dumbly with a head full of jumbled
pictures . . .

'All I can say is, thank God you're here.' But it was
Niccolini who had spoken.

'Me . . .?'

'If you hadn't thought about putting a guard on Moretti's place . . .'

The Marshal didn't answer. The truth was he'd forgotten all about it.

'I'm worried, I don't mind telling you—come on, come on, put your foot down or move over! We just had to pick the moment when everybody and his dog's going home to lunch! I don't like it. I don't like it. You realize that everybody in this town knows what we've just found out? There could be mischief. You're not saying anything. You think I'm exaggerating?'

'No, no . . .'

'Well, you're keeping very quiet. What's the matter with you?' He glanced sideways. 'You look like a broody hen.'

'What?'

'You look like my wife used to look when she was nine months pregnant. Well, all I can hope is that you're brooding over some blinding idea that will solve this little lot for us.'

'I never have ideas.'

'Well, something's up by the look of you. I suppose you're upset by this war business. He can certainly ramble on, can Frasinelli. I must say, though, he made an impression. Funny how often you hear that sort of thing in a general way and think nothing of it. You know what I mean— somebody lets drop some remark, 'So-and-so was killed by the Germans during the war, so-and-so came back from the war and found his wife pregnant by an enemy soldier,' and it doesn't mean a thing, just washes over you. I suppose we were too young. But this business . . . well, it's different when you know the people. All I can say is, I'm glad Moretti has the alibi he has . . . Now, this bridge, for instance.' (They were crossing the bridge that led to the town square, with its bright yellow metal railings.) 'Somebody must have told me once that it had been bombed and this new one built after the war, since I know that's the case, and I

never gave it a thought at the time, but maybe it was the
bad-tempered sergeant and his men who blew it up as they
left—Oh! Will you look at that imbecile! That's right, throw
your hands up in despair because you can't back up now
that all the imbeciles behind have followed you. Bravo!
You've blocked the entire square and we can't turn left! The
trouble with this country is that it's a mass of anarchists and
improvisors governed by bandits. They're moving, thank
goodness. But then, when you think of the Germans maybe
we're better off as we are. I like to think I'm not prejudiced
but when you start thinking . . . Frasinelli's right. I'm
thankful Moretti has an alibi. I wouldn't like to test myself
on this prejudice business . . .'

After a moment the Marshal said, '*We* know he has an
alibi.'

And Niccolini accelerated even more.

'You think like I do, then, that there could be mischief.
That stuff painted on his wall, that was nasty. Even so, you
can understand it, knowing what his father was, whichever
one of them was his father. You know what they say, blood
will tell . . . Well, he has his alibi and that's that.'

They were out of the town centre and speeding past rows
of pots and stacks of tiles and drains when the Marshal
made his next remark almost absent-mindedly since his
head was still full of those jostling images.

'Whose car were they in?'

'Eh?'

'Whose car were they in? Moretti and his clients. They
were driving around together looking at other factories you
said. I wouldn't have thought they'd have taken both his
car and theirs . . .'

'I didn't ask. Why?'

'Because if they took only one . . . when they'd eaten they
must have had to go back to the factory before parting
company. That's where they set out from . . . Either the
clients or Moretti himself had a car to pick up.'

'Good God! And I never even thought to ask. We're here.

Of all the damnfool things, not to think of that. If he came back here right after his lunch—well, that's the first thing to do, ask him. He can't lie to me because I can check up with the clients. Come on!'

He had swung the driver's door open but the Marshal's hand was on his arm.

'Wait.'

'What is it? What's the matter?'

'Wait. Something's wrong.'

'All we have to do is ask him. If they took both cars he's in the clear.'

But the Marshal was staring up at the terrace of the factory, not listening.

'Wait there.'

He got out and looked around. The truck was still parked below the terrace wall, filled with pots with straw packed around them. One big red jar was standing on the wall itself as though there hadn't been room for it. Except for the absence of the men who had been loading the truck and the presence of the carabinieri van parked in front of it everything was as it had been when he'd driven past early that morning. He walked forward and said a word to the two boys in the van, who shrugged and shook their heads. He returned to the car where Niccolini was peering forward, frowning.

'Are you going to tell me? What's up?'

'I don't know. Turn round a minute and stop in front of Robiglio's house.'

Niccolini was too surprised and bemused to protest. They drew up at the gates of Robiglio's house.

'Well?'

There was no one in sight, no face at the window this time, but a white Mercedes was parked in front of the house.

'Is that his car, his only car?'

'No, he has a little runabout mostly used by the maid to do the shopping.'

The Marshal got out and rang the bell beside the gates,

stooping a little to put his ear to the speaker below it.

'Yes?'

'Is Signor Robiglio at home?'

'Yes. Who shall I say?'

'Never mind.'

He straightened up and got back in the car. At the end of the drive they saw the maid open the front door and look in the direction of the gate.

'He's still here,' the Marshal said. 'He made such a point of saying he was leaving for Switzerland this morning and he hasn't gone.'

'Changed his mind,' suggested Niccolini, 'or been delayed.'

'That truck outside Moretti's was as good as packed when I came past this morning, three and a half hours ago. That hasn't gone either.'

'And what does that all mean?'

'I don't know. Go back to Moretti's.'

The Marshal offered no explanations and his face was expressionless behind the sunglasses. A few seconds later they were again parked behind the truck.

'Are we going in?' Niccolini had lost his ebullience in the face of this new version of Guarnaccia. He didn't even protest when he got no answer. They sat where they were with the traffic roaring past.

After a while the Marshal sighed and murmured to himself, 'I don't know . . .'

'What are we going to do?' Niccolini was tapping the steering-wheel again.

'Wait, I suppose . . .'

'Wait for what? We can't sit here for the rest of the day!'

But they hadn't been waiting long when Moretti showed himself on the terrace above them. He remained there staring down for only a few seconds but the Marshal was glad of the chance to take a fresh look at him, seeking to reconcile his idea of the undersized but over-mature orphan of the past with the harassed and defensive man of the present. It wasn't difficult, even in the short time before he vanished again and the terrace was once more deserted except for the tall, big-bellied pot that seemed to be standing guard on the wall.

The Marshal looked about him. On his left the high black wall of the railway line. To his right the factory and behind it an open field with the sherd ruck. He frowned.

'Is there some place at a short distance from where we can keep a watch on this place?'

Niccolini, too, looked about him but came to the same conclusion as the Marshal had done. 'If you mean a place where we can watch without being seen, no.'

'Hmm. And Robiglio's place?'

'Robiglio's. But what . . .'

'Can we keep a watch on that without being seen?'

'Maybe we could from Via del Fosso—'

'Signal to your lads to follow us.'

Niccolini turned the car, seeking an opening in the traffic, and sounded his horn as soon as he could see the van parked beyond the truck. The opening came and both vehicles moved out, turned, and drove past the big gates.

Via del Fosso was a narrow lane leading off to the right, quite a distance beyond Robiglio's house, but it soon began to curve back and climb. They had to stop two or three times before finding a vantage-point which allowed them to see both the back of the house and the front gates.

'That do you?' inquired Niccolini.

'Yes, but take the cars further on and walk back. He's no fool and might spot something even at this distance.'

The Marshal stayed where he was while they concealed the cars, leaning forward a little, his big hands planted wide apart on a low stone wall. Robiglio's house, seen from above, looked rather bigger than he had judged from the façade. He looked at the busy road that passed in front of it and at the electric railway line curving away behind it towards the town. Between the two there was room for a biggish garden and a narrow field.

'Even so,' murmured the Marshal to himself, 'it's not much of a situation for a house of that sort.' It was true that both the road and the railway had obviously been built long after the house.

'And then maybe he'd have trouble selling it just because of that. Still, it's not where I'd choose to live if I had his money, with or without seven lavatories. What a thing to be known for . . . that and fascism.'

'Have a piece of chocolate.' Niccolini had returned and had joined him by the wall.

'Chocolate?'

'Engine can't run without petrol. We haven't eaten all day and though I don't pretend to know what you've got in mind, it doesn't look to me like we're ever going to eat. Here. I always keep a supply in the car. You never know when famine will set in. I've given my lads a block each, they're waiting in the van. Now: what about letting me in on the secret. What's going on?'

'I don't know. I've just got a feeling that something *should* be going on and that we put a stopper on it by having your lads guard Moretti's place all day. I suppose there's nothing to stop anyone loading a truck and leaving it hanging about . . . but Robiglio's hanging about too. They're waiting for something and I just thought maybe they could be waiting for us to be off the scene.'

'And now we are.'

'Yes, now we are. There's something going on between those two, as Dr Frasinelli rightly judged. Something that doesn't suit Moretti or he wouldn't have wanted to make use of that letter . . . There he is.'

The Marshal took off his dark glasses and peered down, blinking.

'Maybe your eyesight's better than mine . . .'

'It's him, all right. Even at this distance I can recognize the way he moves. See him pause at the gates? He's having a good look to make sure we've really gone. What now?'

'We'll go down there, taking our time.'

The Marshal had to repeat the last part of this remark more than once as they made their way down to the main road because Niccolini kept speeding up from fear of what they might miss, and in the end the Marshal ceased exhorting him to slow down, infected by his anxiety and afraid that after all he might have judged the timing badly.

He wasn't sure what exactly he was hoping for, except that perhaps if the two men were closeted in Moretti's office they might overhear something useful. In that he was disappointed. The two men were outside on the terrace above the loaded truck, but they were so deep in a furious argument that they didn't immediately distinguish the noise of the cars drawing up from that of the heavy traffic on the road. The Marshal was out of the car even before Niccolini and in time to hear Moretti's hysterical voice scream out:

'I can't go through with it! I'm in enough trouble already and you can't make me go on. You can't touch me without incriminating yourself!'

'I'll do more than touch you, I'll wipe you out, you and your dirty little factory both!'

The four uniformed men ran up the steps on to the terrace and Niccolini was shouting something, but the two adversaries, whether they noticed or not, were too far gone in their anger to stop themselves, despite the obvious danger of so public a quarrel.

'Try it!' shrieked little Moretti, his face as red as the stains on his ragged clothes and his thin chest heaving. 'Try it and you'll be sorry!'

'Don't delude yourself! A man in my position has nothing to fear from a nobody like you!'

They faced each other squarely as if ready for a fist fight. Between them, on their right, the big-bellied pot stood on the low wall. It had a splash of white glaze on its rim and the Marshal noticed it, thinking of Berti and his white-glazed plates.

'If he sees as much as one spot of glaze on any of his stuff . . .'

He thought maybe that was why it hadn't been packed

with the others, but there was no time to think any further because his view of the pot was blocked by Niccolini who had insinuated himself between the two quarrelling men.

'That'll be enough of that!'

His two lads were flanking Moretti, though without touching his body which was quivering like a live wire. All their eyes were fixed on the slight, red-stained figure and it was a brutal shock when it was Robiglio who burst the group apart, flinging his arms wide in fury.

'Out of my way, blast you! What the devil is this?'

Niccolini, despite his bulk, was thrown sideways while Robiglio's right arm caught the rim of the huge pot and sent it crashing down on to the stack in the truck below. Red sherds flew in all directions and one sharp piece bounced upwards gashing Moretti's cheek. Niccolini recovered his balance quickly and laid a heavy hand on Robiglio's shoulder, but it was brusquely shaken off.

'How dare you lay a hand on me! You'll be hearing from my lawyers!'

'Oh yes? You've got the right idea there, you'll be needing your lawyers before this day's out. In the car, both of you. We're going to talk this over in my office.'

'We're going to do nothing of the sort!'

'No? Well, please yourself. Either you come with me quietly or you come with me under arrest for unlawful assault, wilful damage to the property of Moretti here and outrage to a public official. Suit yourself, but make your mind up. Well?'

The Marshal, observing in silence a few paces away, decided he wouldn't like to be the one to cross Niccolini. His colleague's eyes were glittering dangerously and the veins of his temples were swollen with anger. Perhaps Robiglio came to the same conclusion, because after a few more protests, designed to preserve his dignity rather than to be taken seriously, the group began to move off. Moretti was holding a stained handkerchief to his cheek which was bleeding heavily. The Marshal stood back to let them pass,

but at the top of the steps Moretti hesitated and turned to
look back at the factory.

'I can't . . . I can't just go off like that . . . I'll have to
tell my brother. Someone has to see to things here . . .'

'Go with him,' Niccolini ordered one of his lads, 'and
don't let him out of your sight.'

The rest of them went on down.

As a matter of course, Robiglio and the boy escorting him
approached Niccolini's car. But Niccolini jerked a thumb
towards the van.

'Put him in the back and stay with him.'

'He won't like that,' murmured the Marshal as he got
into the car.

'So he can lump it.' Niccolini had calmed down as suddenly as he had flared up. Now he winked. 'Had too comfortable a life, our friend. He can rough it for once. We'll take
Moretti with us.'

Moretti came down the steps with the young carabiniere
at his heels. Once they were in the car and moving off with
the van turning in their wake, the Marshal sensed so strongly
the silent tension of Moretti behind him that he couldn't
help remembering Dr Frasinelli's account of the child's first
outing from the villa, of how he had sat mute and trembling,
staring straight ahead.

Was that what made the Marshal turn in his seat? It was
true that he glanced at Moretti but he looked back at
the factory too, at where the solitary pot had stood on the
wall, at the ramshackle building beyond, and then at
the tall chimney whose top came into view as the distance
increased.

'Firing again . . .' he murmured, seeing a rising curl of
smoke and he gazed again at Moretti whose eyes seemed in
that moment to become glassy and sightless. Then they
were thrown forward as Niccolini slammed his foot on the
brake. The van almost rammed them from behind. A series
of angry horns sounded in response to the blocked road but
Niccolini jumped out and held up his hand.

'Guarnaccia! Come with me!' He paused a moment to yank open the rear door and thrust his face in at the young carabiniere who stared up at him in amazement.

'I told you not to let him out of your sight!'

'But I didn't. He just spoke to his brother like he said—'

'And told him to light the kiln?'

'Yes . . .'

'Guarnaccia!'

They had to stop the traffic coming the other way too, so they could make a dash for the other side of the road. It would have taken longer to turn the car. They ran back, thudding heavily along in silence, the Marshal panting in Niccolini's wake, only catching him up on the steps of the terrace.

There was no one in the kiln room and no time to waste finding any one. Niccolini turned off all the gas taps he could see and began dismantling the bricked-up door with his gloved hands. The bricks hadn't been cemented up with clay and they were barely warm.

'Firing again! He hasn't a damn thing ready to fire except what he wants to hide. Get some water!'

There was no tap in the room and the Marshal hurried next door in the hope of finding a sink. There sat the silent man who worked alone turning at his wheel, feet buried in the dark red parings. He might never have moved since the Marshal had last passed through. He didn't move now but followed the Marshal with his eyes without pausing in his work.

'Hurry up!' Niccolini's big voice echoed in the high rooms.

The only bucket the Marshal could find had red slurry in the bottom of it, but he dashed water into it anyway and hauled it back to the kiln room. Niccolini grasped it and tossed the water through the hole he'd made, coughing at the smoke and steam that issued from it.

Once they could get near enough they dismantled more of the loose brickwork so as to get inside.

'Whatever it is,' Niccolini said as they peered through the

gloom at a steaming mound in the middle of the kiln floor,
'it's not the scrap of missing clothing I'd expected.'

'No . . .'

It wasn't clothing. The mound had been mostly burned
away but what little was left was easy enough to identify,
despite the muddy red water that discoloured it, as a stack
of banknotes.

The Marshal walked slowly up and down the corridor with
a coffee-cup in his hand. It was after five o'clock in the
afternoon and someone had switched on the lights a moment
ago without his having noticed it. Each time he passed by
the door of Niccolini's office he heard the Captain's voice,
grave and persistent, interrupted on occasion by Niccolini's
more agitated tones but only rarely by a response from
Moretti. Behind the next door a more heated discussion was
in progress between the finance police, who had just arrived,
and Robiglio and his lawyer. The Marshal was aware of
these voices as he passed each door but he wasn't listening
to them. Anyone seeing him walking slowly back and forth,
his great eyes fixed on the empty corridor before him, would
have said he was thinking hard. In fact, his mind was a
blank. In any case no one had time to bother watching him
since the little Station had never in all its days seen so much
action as in the last few hours. If things seemed quieter now
it was mainly because Robiglio had calmed down a good
deal, probably on the advice of his lawyer, in the time it
had taken for the Captain to arrive from Florence with the
two men from the finance police and be brought up to date.
Before that, Niccolini had made the mistake of talking to
Robiglio and Moretti together about the stack of banknotes.
When Robiglio had realized that the money had been
burned he had jumped on little Moretti and hit him viciously
in the eye before they'd been able to stop him. After that
they'd been kept waiting in separate rooms and Moretti, his
cheek bandaged and the new cut on his eyebrow bleeding
slightly, had begun spilling the beans to Niccolini and the

Marshal, though only to the extent of trying to incriminate Robiglio while protecting himself. He admitted that Robiglio had asked him to export the money which was the proceeds of illegal gambling, and that Robiglio had intended to collect it once it had crossed the border. He even explained that it was to have been packed under straw in the marked pot which in the end had never been loaded.

'Why wasn't it?'

'Because your men arrived and parked themselves right in front of my place.'

'Otherwise you'd have done as he asked?'

'No!'

'Come on, Moretti, you'd accepted the money and the pot was already marked.'

'He was trying to force me, but I wouldn't have done it. I didn't do it, and you can't prove otherwise.'

'You didn't do it because my men were there, you said so yourself. Nevertheless you had the money in your possession and that's going to take some explaining away when the finance people get here.'

'It wasn't my money. He left it there.'

'Without your knowledge?'

'Yes.'

'But you knew where to lay your hands on it when you panicked and decided to burn it.'

'It's not true.'

'You put it in the kiln.'

'I didn't. He must have put it there!'

'So you told your brother to light the kiln with nothing in it? A bit extravagant, that. Stop wasting my time, Moretti. That was how you paid him off for the orchard, wasn't it? For your sister's dowry?'

'No.'

'How did you pay him, then? You were in debt at the time.'

'I paid in instalments.'

'You have the receipts?'

'He didn't give me any receipts.'

'Very trusting of you. You have the cheque stubs at least?'

'I . . . no. I paid him in cash.'

'How often? Once a month?'

'No—yes, once a month.'

'In that case we can check with your bank and they'll be able to show us the withdrawals that correspond with these payments.'

'No! No . . . I didn't . . . I paid him directly from money coming into the business.'

'You have clients who pay cash? Well, well. Still, it will be no trouble to check your invoices and see what the amount was that didn't find its way to the bank. How much?'

'How much . . .?'

'That's right, how much were you paying him each month?'

'I . . . I don't remember. It varied.'

'Varied?'

'Depending on what I could afford . . .'

'What a generous and understanding man our friend Robiglio must be! Who'd have thought it? You're a fool, Moretti, do you know that? You never paid him anything because you couldn't afford it. You exported Robiglio's gambling proceeds regularly and for each run you did he knocked a certain sum off your debt for the orchard.'

'It's not true.'

At that point the Marshal had left them to it and gone into the duty room to see if one of the lads there could get him a cup of coffee. He felt exhausted and it looked like being a long time before he would be able to get away. He was also both depressed and disturbed. Depressed because, however much Moretti might have been at fault, the fact was that his chances now depended not on himself and his greater or lesser guilt but upon the skill of Robiglio's lawyer and the line he decided to take. If he could extricate Robiglio and plant the whole thing on Moretti, he would. But the business of the orchard, the quarrel in front of witnesses, and the black eye inflicted right here in Niccolini's office had pretty well put paid to that. Probably his only hope was to maintain that there was no case to answer, which meant that they had to pull Moretti out of the mire along with Robiglio. Neither solution was what the Marshal would call justice. Well, it wasn't his problem, he could only do his job to the best of his ability.

What was disturbing him was the thought that he hadn't even done that. Even if it was true, as the Captain thought, that the Swiss girl had found out about the goings-on in the factory, there was a lot to be explained on that score. The body being dumped on the sherd ruck, for instance. It might have pointed to Moretti or it might have been meant to point to Moretti. But after seeing the money burning in an empty kiln it was impossible not to think that the sherd ruck might have been a temporary measure because the murder had coincided with a firing that could hardly have been delayed without arousing suspicion. Once the pots were unloaded . . . perhaps during the night—But no, it was too bizarre, too calculated! A body might be tossed down a well, or into a river, or almost anywhere in the heat and panic following a murder, but a thing like that, only a madman would do it.

The Marshal ceased striding up and down, pausing for a moment to lean his forehead against the cold glass of the corridor's one window, which overlooked the square. It was quite dark by now and an icy wind was sending flurries of fine moisture against the window. They clung for a second before melting into drops. The beginnings of the first snow. Below in the lamplit square the bronze head of the partisan gleamed a dark orange. The Marshal's body tensed as he set his cup on the windowsill and peered down, frowning. There was something odd about the statue. A placard of some kind had been hung about its neck. It wasn't possible for the Marshal to see what was written there, but as his

eyes became accustomed to the darkness he realized that
the square was full of people. He hadn't noticed them before
but the reason for that was that they were standing quite
still in big groups. Many of them were staring up at the
windows of the barracks. He could hear nothing, which
made their presence all the more sinister. There was no
knowing how long they had been out there in the freezing
November darkness, but there could be no doubt that the
anonymous letter-writers were among them. There might
well also be some of those who had once stood in that same
square on a warm summer morning when the flies had been
settling on the mangled corpse of Pietro Moro. The Marshal
shivered. It had seemed unlikely that anyone but a madman
could have tried to rape and then strangled an innocent girl
and planned to burn the body in a kiln, but there was no
denying that there might well be a madman out there among
that silent threatening crowd. Out there, not in here. Moretti
was no madman, surely . . . and though he was wiry, he
was so small. How could he have killed a big healthy girl
without her at least managing to scratch his face for him?
Robiglio was a much bigger man, a man who had brushed
aside the hefty Niccolini like a fly that was bothering him.
But that meant following the Captain's line . . . and the
rape, or attempt at it? He'd said himself to that smooth
young man Corsari, 'Somebody didn't take too kindly to
being teased the way she teased . . .' But a normal man
didn't rape and kill for that. Even so, there was Robiglio
the fascist to bear in mind . . . the things he'd done during
the war. Were those things normal? Where do you draw the
line?

   He had begun walking up and down again and now he
stopped and opened the door of Niccolini's office. He felt he
needed to take another look at Moretti, as if to reassure
himself. He slipped in quietly and sat himself down in a
corner near the rubber plant. The Captain was plodding
patiently and systematically through a series of questions
based on the notes he had taken during the earlier briefing

session. It didn't sound as though he was getting anywhere. The atmosphere was just as the Marshal had left it some time before, cold and tense. Niccolini was sitting beside the Captain and one of his boys was typing rapidly with two fingers at a small table in a far corner.

'How did the girl find out? Did she see something? Over-hear something?'

'The girl has nothing to do with it. How could she have? Robiglio only asked me yesterday to take that money up—'

'And the other times?'

'There were no other times.'

The Captain showed signs of impatience.

'What was your relationship with Monica Heer?'

'There was no relationship. I let her come in to throw now and again, nothing else.'

'Isn't it true that you frequently went round to Berti's studio when she was there, that you told your sister you found the girl attractive?'

'No.'

'Your sister told Marshal Guarnaccia here that that was the case.'

'My sister isn't normal. Besides, I never see her. I used to, but I don't like the way her husband treats her and my visits always caused trouble.'

'According to her, she often comes to see you, on Thurs-days when her husband is out playing billiards.'

'It's not true. I see her twice a year, at Christmas and Easter. It wouldn't be fair to my wife to have her around more often, or to my little girl.'

'Her words were, I quote: "I go to see my brother, he lets me talk to him."'

'I've told you, my sister's not normal.'

'A great many other things she told us turned out to be true.'

'I can't help that. She never sets foot in my house except twice a year. You can ask my wife.'

'So she never sets foot in your house. Does she come round to the factory to see you?'

'On Thursday nights when her husband's out playing billiards? I finish work and go home at six, six-thirty at the latest. Any of my men can confirm that.'

'Then what about something your men can't confirm. On the day the girl was murdered you came back to the factory after lunching with your clients.'

'I went home!'

'You went home, but you first went back to the factory either to collect your car or to deliver your clients to theirs. We don't yet know which, but we'll know tomorrow when we telephone the clients themselves.'

'It doesn't mean I went in.'

'Whose car did you go back to collect?'

'Mine.'

'The girl was in there alone, working. She too had just had lunch, according to the autopsy, her last lunch, a sandwich. Did you know she was in there?'

'No!'

'I think you did. I think you were round at Berti's on the Friday before and that's how she knew you were firing. She knew in advance because she got off the bus and walked straight to your place without waiting for Berti to turn up. She must have known.'

'If she knew before Berti must have told her!'

'Somebody must have told him, then. I understand you fire his pots.'

'Yes.'

'So who told him you were ready to fire?'

'Anybody could have told him! And anybody could have got into my place and done for that girl. Anybody! The place is never locked!'

There was a faint rustle in the vicinity of the rubber plant as the Marshal got to his feet, but no one noticed it. It was almost half an hour later, when the Substitute Prosecutor had been called and asked to make out a warrant and

Moretti was holding out his wrists for the handcuffs to be put on them, that the Captain looked about him and then flung open the door to shout down the corridor.

'Where the devil's Guarnaccia!'

CHAPTER 9

'Report's ready, Captain.' The boy in the doorway was breathless, as though he'd been running rather than typing in a rush.

'Thank you—no, no, take this to Marshal Niccolini for his signature.'

'He's downstairs, sir, trying to do something about the crowd outside.'

'Then wait till he comes up.' Captain Maestrangelo turned back to the Substitute Prosecutor. 'What do you think?'

'His lawyer's no fool. I'd say we could hold him under house arrest for the moment. I wouldn't try to go further until you have more evidence. Now, this other man—what's his name?'

'Moretti.'

'Hm. You're sure of your ground?'

'The evidence is largely circumstantial but he's virtually confessed on both counts, a partial confession. Given time . . .'

'Then hold him for forty-eight hours and make your decision on what charge you want to arrest him on. I've had seals put on the kiln and the technicians will collect the remains of the money tomorrow, though I imagine it won't be traceable—'

'Excuse me, sir!' This time the boy really had been running.

'What is it?'

'Marshal Niccolini needs us downstairs. He's trying to clear the piazza but he's having difficulty.'

'Then all of you go down except the radio operator and he can call in the patrol bikes.' He followed the boy out into the corridor, 'And tell Marshal Niccolini the Substitute wants a word with him before he leaves.'

Then he saw Guarnaccia. He had just come in, bringing a blast of cold air with him, and was standing there holding his hat which had fine icy particles on it, as had the shoulders of his black greatcoat.

'Where the devil have you been?' the Captain asked irritably but under his breath so as not to let the Substitute hear.

'I had to speak to Moretti's wife . . .' The Marshal made no move to unbutton his coat but went on standing there, his face wooden.

'That could have waited. We have enough on our hands here. Niccolini could have done with your help down here.'

'They're moving on now. Have you arrested Moretti?'

'We're holding him for forty-eight hours. You'd better join us in Niccolini's office if you think you're not needed downstairs.'

'Where is he now?'

'Moretti? In the cells.'

'I think I'd better speak to him . . .'

The Captain was about to lose his temper but checked himself in time. He'd seen that expression, or rather lack of it, on Guarnaccia's face before.

'Is something the matter?'

'No . . . no . . . Everything's all right now. I didn't do a very good job on this business, though. I'm not competent . . . should have thought on . . . If you don't mind, I'd better go out again when I've seen Moretti.' He was putting on his hat and the Captain realized that he wasn't asking for permission to go, he was going, as oblivious of his superior officer's presence as if he hadn't seen him. Indeed, he really seemed to be talking to himself as he turned and pushed open the door to the stairs.

'It struck me right away the first time he said that about

the place never being locked but then I forgot about it . . . made a bit of a fool of myself.'

And he was gone.

Niccolini was thundering up the stairs, taking them two at a time and shouting to the young carabiniere behind who was keeping up with difficulty: 'By God, I'd have put a few of them inside if I'd had the space—and I'd give a lot to know who informed the newspapers—ah! Guarnaccia! So there you are! What's going on? Where are you off to this time?'

And he turned to stare after the Marshal who was stumping off past them down the stairs muttering something incomprehensible under his breath.

There were only two cells in the dimly lit basement. Moretti was in the one on the left, seated on the end of the narrow bed facing the bars, his head in his hands. He looked up when he heard the Marshal's footsteps, his face a deathly colour and his heart beating visibly in the thin chest.

'I've been to see your wife.'

'How is she?'

'Fairly calm, all things considered.'

'Did she . . . did she say anything?'

'Not much. She didn't need to. It'll all come out in time. I didn't insist. She did admit when I asked her that she'd called in your next-door neighbour on your advice so that you'd all be seen having coffee together. I didn't ask her much apart from that.'

Moretti stared into the Marshal's impassive face.

'You know, don't you?'

'I know. Who else does?'

'For sure, only Sestini . . .'

'You'd have done well to listen to his advice instead of fighting with him.'

'He doesn't understand, nobody understands.'

'I think you're wrong there; nevertheless, there's an innocent girl dead. Sestini was right to attack you, but after all, he didn't give you away so you're doing him an injustice in saying he doesn't understand.'

'You try to help people, you do what you can . . .'

'But some people are beyond help. Now the best thing you can do is to help us.'

'I can't . . .' Moretti's head dropped into his hands again and he began rocking himself to and fro like a distressed child.

The Marshal regarded him for a moment, noting for the first time that the red hair was greying at the temples. Then he said quietly, 'No, no . . . you're right. For once, somebody has to help you.'

He saw that Moretti seemed to be breathing with difficulty and wondered about his heart.

'I should lie down for a bit, if I were you.' But the hunched figure didn't move.

Outside in the piazza everything was quiet. The only remaining sign of the disturbance was the placard which still hung around the neck of the partisan's statue, saying: COME DOWN PIETRO MORO WE STILL NEED YOU HERE. No doubt there would be a photograph of it in next morning's paper. The Marshal got into his car and drove off. Niccolini was right, prejudice was a frightening business. Nobody had had anything against Moretti all these years but as soon as he was in trouble everybody remembered his German blood.

In the darkness he almost missed the factory, only pulling over just in time. He got out of the car. It was a deserted spot even in the daytime, apart from the continuous passing of trucks, and now there was no sound except the keen November wind that howled around the tall chimney silhouetted against a starry sky. He had to feel his way up the steps in the darkness. The door was closed but only with a wooden bar which lifted easily. Once inside, he stumbled against some bags of clay and it took him some time feeling about on the inside wall to locate a light switch. It occurred to him then that there was very likely another entrance, but he didn't fancy groping about outside in the freezing cold looking for it. It was cold enough in here. He went from room to room as quietly as he could, switching on lights and looking about him. He found his way to the kiln and saw that the opening in the front of the kiln had been filled up with loose bricks again and seals put on it. In the next room he was almost surprised not to find the silent little man working at his turning wheel. His overall lay there, draped over his stool, and the imprint of his boots was clearly visible in the leathery red ribbons piled around the wheel's base. The Marshal's footsteps were loud on the bare brick floor. He didn't switch off the lights behind him as he proceeded, uncomfortable at the idea of leaving all that empty darkness in his wake. It even occurred to him that perhaps it hadn't been such a good idea to come here alone. Nevertheless, he kept on walking steadily.

In the room where the throwers worked more stained overalls hung over the seats of the wheels which had been washed clean at the end of the day's work. A dozen or so newly thrown pots were lined up on a wooden table, identical, their sides still smooth and wet. This time, when he came to the wooden staircase, he didn't turn and go up. He was pretty sure that he would find what he was looking for on the ground floor. Unfortunately, once beyond the stairs he was in a part of the factory which was new to him and pretty soon he lost his bearings. Once, when he opened a door and found the light already on he stopped short, his nerves tingling, only to find it was a room he'd already been through, which meant the corridor he'd followed had brought him back almost to the stairs from where he'd set out. There was no mistaking it; he'd already seen those big baths of water with the dark clay settled well beneath the surface, and the long table in the centre with some sort of tubular machine with a polythene bag tied over the end of it. He turned back. He was doing his best to walk quietly but in such dead silence it was impossible. He wandered about for some time before finding a door he was sure he hadn't tried before. It was a makeshift door of planks that had rotted away near the bottom, no doubt because of the

dampness that oozed from all the clay in this area. There
was no lock or handle and only a bit of string looped round
a nail in the doorpost held it more or less shut. He opened
it slowly to avoid its creaking too much and then gazed
beyond into total darkness. No amount of feeling about
the rough walls on either side of what must have been a
passageway produced a light switch. It would be at the
other end. There was nothing for it but to make do with
such light as came from the room behind him. By the time
his eyes were accustomed to the gloom he found himself half
way along a dusty tiled passage which made his footfall even
louder than before, despite all his efforts.

'Who's here?'

He stopped dead. The voice had come from behind a door
at the far end. Without answering, he walked right up to it
and knocked.

'Who is it? Tina?'

The voice sounded thick and slow as though the speaker
had been woken from a deep sleep.

'Open up, Moretti.' Was it the mention of Tina that made
him add, 'I've come to talk to you.'

There was no answer, but a creaking noise suggested that
someone was sitting up in bed.

'Don't be afraid, I'm coming in to talk to you.'

As he had expected, the door wasn't locked. He opened
it quietly.

It seemed only natural that it should be the kitchen.
There must have been other rooms to this corner where the
family had once lived, but this was the room that Dr
Frasinelli's story had prepared him for, and in essence it
was just as he'd thought it would be. A rusted black stove
stood against the back wall, a heavy, scuffed sideboard was
piled high with junk of every description, and the wooden
table in the centre held a flask of wine and a dirty glass, and
at one end a big lump of clay with a roughly modelled head
beside it. The face was grotesque and open-mouthed, like
the ones he had seen that first day on the window ledge by

the kiln. The Marshal's big eyes travelled over it all quickly. In its present state of chaos the room spoke too much of the violence it had seen, of Maria sprawled on the disordered table. There were no bloodstains splashed on the wall now, only the yellow stains of damp and neglect. In the corner stood an old iron bedstead and a bulky figure huddled there, half covered by a worn and colourless blanket.

'Moretti . . .' murmured the Marshal, meeting the small frightened eyes embedded in heavy flesh. He hadn't known what face to put to the name until seeing it, but now he recognized the woollen cap on the floor by the bed, lying next to a pair of clay-spattered boots with one of the laces missing. The man's head was completely bald. He had aged as prematurely as his sister.

The little eyes watched him warily like those of a wild animal undecided whether to attack or flee.

'My brother said you wouldn't come for me. He said he wouldn't tell.'

'He didn't tell. Is this where you live all the time, not with your brother?'

'I like it here. I go to my brother's to eat and watch television but I like it better here. I have to look after the factory.'

Little wonder that Moretti felt no need to lock the place up with this creature on guard. The man seemed sunk in a sort of torpor and showed no open resentment at this intrusion. Nevertheless, the Marshal remained standing near the door and didn't venture any closer to the rumpled bed.

'What are you going to do to me?'

'Nothing. Nobody's going to hurt you. Perhaps you should get dressed.'

The hulk in the bed moved slowly and the blanket fell aside. He was wearing long woollen underwear, yellowish with age and stained at the wrists and neck with red clay. He sat himself on the edge of the narrow bed, which creaked under his weight, and bent forward, but he didn't reach for his clothes that lay in a heap against the wall, only fished out some cigarettes and matches from underneath. The Marshal observed him with some trepidation. The man was built like an ox and it was evident that such a mass of muscle would have no difficulty in shifting great bags of sodden clay as the Marshal had seen him do, or in crushing the life out of a young girl . . . At school they had called him Big Beppe . . .

Big Beppe lit a cigarette. His hands were perfectly steady but still he looked about him as though dazed.

'You'd better get dressed,' the Marshal repeated gently.

'What for? You said you wouldn't do anything to me. It wasn't my fault. Ask my brother.'

'We will ask him. I want you to come with me now and talk to him. He needs your help.'

The other only stared at him dully, not understanding.

'You helped him once before, do you remember? A long time ago when you were both at school and the others were teasing him. You helped him and now you have to help him again.'

Perhaps he didn't remember the incident. At any rate, he sat where he was, smoking and scratching his broad chest. After a moment he repeated with sullen intensity, 'It wasn't my fault.'

The Marshal risked coming closer and laid a hand on Big Beppe's solid shoulder. 'It will all get sorted out. But first we'll go and see your brother.'

A sick odour of sweat and clay rose from the big body. He saw the corner of a magazine sticking out from under the blanket. There was no need to see more of it to know what it was.

'Your sister comes to see you here, doesn't she?'

'She comes to talk to me.'

'And brings you those magazines?'

'She gets them from Berti. He . . .'

'What about him?'

'He said the girl would . . . He said she'd do it with anybody but that she liked me.'

'Did you go there often, to Berti's studio to see the girl?'

'She always smiled at me. She liked talking to me, and Berti said . . . he told me things he'd done to her, right there in the studio.'

'He was lying, Moretti. Do you understand? He was only teasing you.'

'No, it's not true. She was there and she heard him.'

'But she didn't understand him.'

'The things he said—'

'She didn't understand. She was a foreigner and wouldn't understand a lot of what was said.'

The Marshal noticed thankfully that he had started, as if absent-mindedly, to fumble with the pile of clothes.

'She liked me, so why did she . . . Berti said she'd come to see me and she did.'

'She came to work, Moretti, that's all. Berti was having you on.'

'You don't understand. She liked me. I told her she could come in here and eat her sandwiches. I made her some coffee. If she did it with everybody else, why not with me? I didn't mean to hurt her, only to keep her still. It wasn't my fault, you can ask my brother. I wasn't going to tell anybody. Nobody would have known, but then my brother came back and saw . . . He was angry. He said what's done is done and he took me home with him. He knows I didn't want to hurt her, you can ask him.'

'We will, we'll talk to your brother.'

'He always said he'd find somebody for me. He found somebody for Tina. I wanted somebody of my own.'

'Put your boots on, and your hat—it's cold.'

Why should his lack of a bootlace be the thing that banished the Marshal's fear and aroused his compassion? All the more so because he knew that in any case they would shortly take the other one from him.

'Take your cigarettes.'

A brief flash of animal cunning crossed Big Beppe's face.

'But you'll be bringing me back soon!'

'Of course. But you might want a smoke while we're talking.'

The face became docile and stupid again. The Marshal's heart was heavy with the misery of it all, for this dumb beast of a man, for the body of a pretty girl soiled and broken under a pile of sherds, for frail, fierce little Moretti, dumped by a war of which he knew nothing into a situation like this.

'Let's go.'

Seeing him pull back a bit of torn curtain that concealed the kitchen's own entrance, the Marshal stopped him.

'We have to go out through the factory. I left all the lights on.' He led the way himself back along the tiled corridor. They were at the foot of the stairs and he had just turned out the light when he heard the footsteps behind him stop. He paused, feeling his scalp prickling under his hat.

'What is it?'

'You're not going to lock me up in the villa?'

'We're just going to talk to your brother.'

'Because once when I hit Sestini—my brother told me, he said it wasn't my fault and that they wouldn't torment me any more, he'd see to that, but that if I hurt anybody they'd lock me up in the villa!'

'Don't worry, nobody's going to hurt you.' He walked forward slowly and heard the footsteps follow him. They had passed through the throwing room and were momentarily in darkness when the sound of a siren in the not too far distance caused the Marshal to scent danger. He turned, thinking to get the man in front of him and keep a wary hand on the Beretta in its holster, but before he could complete the turn he felt a vicious blow on his left temple which almost swung him off his feet. Instinctively he lifted his forearm to ward off further blows, only to take a kick in the stomach that made him double up, winded and retching. He could see nothing but buzzing rings of light in a nauseating blackness, but doubled up as he was he began to run, one hand clutching his stomach, the other outstretched to avoid obstacles. Heavy feet were thudding behind him but he knew he was running faster than his pursuer and despite his stunned condition he remembered with gratitude that heavy unlaced boot which might well save his life. Then his right hip crashed into something sharp and solid, stopping him in his tracks and doubling him up further. The pain was so sharp as to make him groan aloud but he silenced himself in an instant as he became aware that the blackness around him was no longer the result of concussion but real darkness, and that the thudding footsteps behind him had stopped. He had run the wrong way in his pain and blindness, away from the light and the exit and into the darkness of a maze he couldn't fathom even in broad daylight. He stood still, trying to quieten the sound of his broken breath. He could hear and see nothing. Gingerly he stretched out a hand. It touched a piece of polythene, the heavy tubular machine, a table.

'You want to lock me in the villa.' The voice was quiet and close. The Marshal didn't answer. A cold sweat broke on his forehead. Would he switch on the light? He was moving about now, the unlaced boot shuffling after the other. What need had he to switch on the light when he spent his every waking moment in the place and probably wandered about it often enough in the dark. Or was it craftiness? He must know the Marshal was armed. And it was true that there was no other way. If there was no light he would have to wait for the voice again and shoot at it. Very slowly he let his right hand drop until it touched the leather of his holster. He slid the Beretta out without even the faintest noise.

'What are you doing?'

The Marshal raised his arm, sprung the first bullet and fired. A scream of rage and pain told him the shot had gone home but had only wounded. Then he was flung backwards and big hands closed over his throat. He tried to use his own weight to push his attacker off but he was off balance right from the start and was driven backwards until his legs hit something sharp which he knew must be one of the big baths of clay. He was still holding the Beretta and now he hit out with it, fired it again and heard the bullet rebound from something metallic. The grip on his throat was inexorable and he knew that he must soon lose consciousness. With a last desperate effort he managed to draw up one knee and push. Even as he did it he realized it was a mistake and probably his last, for it only overbalanced him more, levering him backwards over the edge of the bath so that the water closed over his ears making them sing. His eyes were still open but he was losing his sense of reality and couldn't be sure if he saw or imagined the tiny eyes gleaming close to his face. Then his head plunged backwards under the water and into the slimy clay below. Through the singing and bubbling in his ears he heard a spent scream and in his last conscious moment was lucid enough to wonder whether it was his own.

CHAPTER 10

'Imbecile!' roared Niccolini, raising his fist, 'imbecile! Is this what you wanted? To finish up in this place? You must have gone out of your mind—I still can't believe you did it! You should be under restraint, by God, you should be— Here's a bit of chocolate for you—not to mention giving me the trouble of driving all this way just to tell you what a jackass you are!'

'How did you get in?'

'I have my methods. How are you feeling?'

'Well—'

'Good. It's more than you deserve.'

The Marshal smiled. He'd been about to say that he was feeling worse than he'd ever felt in his life, but if he couldn't combat Niccolini's steam-roller conversation at the best of times he wasn't going to try it from a hospital bed.

'Now then.' Niccolini sat down on the bed, making it

bounce and the Marshal wince. 'The best thing you can do is to get yourself out of this place as fast as you can. Go about tackling ten-ton maniacs on your own if you must, but at least keep away from quacks who'll finish you off in no time once you let them start.'

'They're keeping me here another week under observation.'

'Rubbish! You really must learn to defend yourself—and in more ways than one.'

'I'm afraid you're right. How did I . . . how was it that he didn't manage . . .?'

'You don't know? You mean nobody's told you anything?'

'Nobody. They won't let anybody in except my wife and she's under orders not to mention work to me. They say complete rest . . .'

'And how are you supposed to rest if you don't know what's going on! No sense in it at all. Well, it's true you were in a bad way and it's not a pleasant business to talk about, but the long and the short of it is Big Beppe's dead. We got there just in time, but we had a devil of a job finding you in that place. It's lucky for you that you fired, otherwise . . . But surely you heard our sirens?'

'It was you? I knew I'd hit him but I didn't think—I killed him, then. That's what they didn't want to tell me.'

'Nothing of the sort.' Niccolini's face darkened a little. 'I shot him. Had no choice. Nobody could have got him off you any other way and it was a matter of seconds . . . To tell you the truth, I thought you were a goner as it was. It's not a thing I've ever had to do before and I hope I never have to do it again, but there it is.'

'Then you saved my life.'

'Nothing of the kind. Little Moretti saved your life. He asked for me after you'd gone. Nobody else knew what you were up to but apparently he did—did you tell him?'

'I told him I knew . . .'

'Well, he must have got scared and what he wanted to tell me was not to go for Beppe unless he went with us because nobody else could control him if he got violent. It seems Moretti wouldn't let him in his own house unless he was there himself—that's why he stayed at the factory that lunch-time when Moretti ate with his clients. Anyway, at that point it didn't take much working out where you'd slipped off to, so I went after you with a couple of my lads. I'll tell you something else you don't know: a few years back there was an incident at the factory—the men had been teasing Big Beppe as they often did and he reacted and went for Sestini, nearly did for him. It was lucky Moretti was there, otherwise . . . Anyway, the matter was settled between themselves and no report made to us. They never teased him again after that.'

The Marshal didn't say that he already knew something of the story. Nor did he mention that if the men of the factory had given up teasing Big Beppe, Berti hadn't. He didn't feel up to going into all that yet and there was no longer any urgency. He was sufficiently satisfied to know that after being so ambivalent for so long in his attitude to Berti he could now settle on disliking him thoroughly, though he remained fascinated by his skill in the way a bird might be fascinated by a snake.

'Well, there it is,' concluded Niccolini, rousing himself to be cheerful again. 'I'm only glad I didn't have time to think before doing what had to be done. After all, the poor creature would otherwise have ended his days up at the villa and I think that would have broken little Moretti's heart after all he'd done to prevent it.'

'How is he?'

'He'll do. He has his wife and little girl and the factory to keep him busy. Of course there's still a case to answer, this business of Robiglio's money.'

'Will it come to anything?'

'Not if I know Robiglio. After all, Moretti only confessed to the one incident, and the money never left. Robiglio's lawyers will get him off—he's under house arrest for the moment but that character has nine lives. He got himself back in power after the war and I reckon he'll soon be strutting about the town as if nothing had happened. He'll rise to the top again, scum always does. The only consolation is that he won't be standing for election any more, not this time, at least.'

'But there'll be a next time.'

'Oh, there'll be a next time all right. Sooner or later we'll be blessed with him as mayor. Well, I hope I get transferred before it happens. Who's standing in for you, by the way?'

'My brigadier can manage, he's a competent lad.'

They chatted for a while of everyday problems but it was inevitable that their thoughts should return before long to the case that was uppermost in their minds.

'Did you ever find the missing clothing?' the Marshal asked.

'Not a sign. We searched Big Beppe's den but I imagine it was got rid of right away either by him or Moretti.'

'Did her parents ever come down?'

'No. The body leaves tomorrow by train. The Captain saw to everything from here. I gather the other lass is to travel with the body. It's been a bad shock for her, I shouldn't wonder. Was she as pretty as her friend?'

'No, she wasn't pretty, but she struck me as a good-hearted, affectionate creature, if a bit strange.'

He wondered where someone in her situation could turn for comfort. Probably not even to her parents from whom she had most likely hidden the truth. He thought of that young man Corsari, neither flesh nor fowl, who had made a friend of both girls. The thought gave him no pleasure.

Niccolini, determined to keep a cheerful note, had launched into the story of another of his past conquests. He had just come to the climax of the story, his voice loud and his eyes bright, when the door burst open and an angry young nurse appeared.

'What's going on in here? I could hear the noise from the far end of the corridor! I thought you had two minutes' business to transact.'

'Perfectly right. All finished now. I was just leaving—'

'Do you realize that this patient has three cracked ribs, a chipped femur and a damaged throat? Not to mention shock and drowning! I must ask you to leave immediately. The doctor's on his way.' She swept out, closing the door with an angry click.

'Beautiful girl,' remarked Niccolini, his eyes still bright. 'Plenty of spirit, too, which I always like. Is that why you're content to hang around here for another week? Well, I suppose I'd better leave you. But having come all this way to tell you what a jackass you are, I might as well tell you that I was pretty impressed as well that you got on to the truth the way you did. To be quite honest, when I first met you I thought you were going to be a dead loss. You won't be offended? I thought to myself: This chap's asleep on his feet. You give that impression—you're not offended?'

'No, no . . .' He was a little offended. Goodness knows, he was used to it. Ever since his earliest schooldays people had got angry with him for seeming asleep on his feet. His wife often complained of it, too. But he was sorry to have made such an impression on his new friend and wished he had a quarter of his energy and cheerfulness.

'I'm glad you came,' he told Niccolini as the latter grasped his hand and shook it vigorously, not without some ill effect on those cracked ribs.

'You take my advice and get home as fast as you can— and take another piece of advice: don't go risking your neck like that again! It's not worth it. You'd have done nobody any good by getting yourself killed. Doing your duty's all very well but don't take it all too seriously, you've your own life to live and enjoy. Advice finished. I'm off. All the best!'

When he had gone the room was heavy with silence and the Marshal was left to concentrate on the combined pains of his broken bones and swollen throat and a thorough dissatisfaction with himself. He'd never much minded being thought dozy before, but all of a sudden he minded it very much. Could it be a question of diet? Perhaps he ate the wrong sort of thing. His glance fell on the huge bar of chocolate on the locker beside him. It must have weighed a kilo. Sugar was probably a good thing for giving you energy. With some difficulty he managed to stretch out an arm and get hold of the chocolate. Even breaking a piece off hurt him, but he did it and settled down to munch thoughtfully. While he had so much time to spare he should make out a new plan for his life, beginning with being more careful about what he ate and an attempt at making a better impression on people by being more lively and communicative. He would start right away while he was still in the hospital. He could discuss this business of diet with the doctor, be a lot more chatty to that pretty nurse who probably thought him the dullest patient ever to be wished on her, and show a bit more interest in all the little things his wife chattered about in the hope of cheering him up.

Ten minutes later the nurse entered followed by his wife and the doctor, and the three of them stood around his bed looking down at him. The nurse had no intention of admitting that she had let in an unlawful visitor to exhaust her patient and she was careful to say as she felt for his pulse, 'As you see, he's in much less pain today.'

The Marshal responded with a gentle snore.

Magdalen Nabb has lived in Florence since 1975.
Originally a potter, she now writes full time.